THE WATCHERS

HIDDEN FIRE

DEIRDRA EDEN

THE WATCHERS SERIES

Dedicated To:

My dear husband, Leif.

The Watchers books wouldn't be as romantic

or exciting without you in my life to inspire me.

Chapter One

The Resister

England - 1276 A.D.

A few years after Auriella's knighting.

The Shadow Legion's stink of decay and burning sulfur washed over me like the perfume of death.

The candles around the tub flickered. I pulled the silk robe tighter around my naked body. The cloth clung to the back of my wet legs. I searched the mirror's reflection, keeping my breath steady.

From behind the curtains, the Shadow Lord's hungry eyes flashed in the mirror and fixed on me. His gaze revealed a lust to steal the power running through my blood. It didn't matter how many Watchers the Shadow Legion killed—their feral craving for power could never be satisfied.

I watched the creature in the mirror. The severely decaying body was a sign of his desperate state. His bulging eyes were wide open, like someone had pinned back his eyelids with sewing needles.

I whirled to face him. There was nothing but a breeze blowing through the curtains of the open window. The lamplights enhanced the wall of steam floating from the tub and across the stone floor. I tried to see through the shroud of eerie fog.

The curtains shifted unnaturally. I narrowed my eyes. "There you are." My skin tingled as heat burst from my heart and traveled through my veins. I stretched out my hand, releasing the adrenaline-charged surge of energy in the direction of the Shadow Lord. The curtains erupted in flames and dropped to the ground in a smoldering heap.

The explosion briefly distorted the light in the room, making the oil lamps look like dim stars around the sun. Footsteps pounded across the ceiling. My hands tightened into flaming fists. I hated these creatures' ability to scale walls and skitter across the ceiling like spiders. The next strike could come from anywhere.

I pressed my back against the stone wall. I scanned the ceiling and searched the dark corners for the Shadow Lord. Neither of us had the element of surprise now. The flames that crowned the candles around the tub danced, making the shadows flicker. I tightened my jaw, clenching it so hard that my ears popped.

A blade whistled metallically through the air as it propelled toward me. I lunged as it glinted past me. Copper sparks scattered as the weapon struck stone. The dagger spun across the floor, whirling like a top from the momentum of the throw.

Flames shot up my arms and danced across my skin. "Are you afraid to face me?" I challenged. I wanted to get this fight over with. If I was late to another of the king's victory celebrations, he would probably have me hanged.

It wasn't like I planned these attacks; they always came with very little warning. I had thought for sure I would be safe in my own washroom. The Shadow Legion hated water and avoided it at all cost. Of course, water was my weakness as well. The fire I summoned to protect and heal me couldn't be wielded under the liquid surface.

The Shadow Lord dropped from the ceiling and snatched the dagger from the floor. I tried not to look startled at his misshapen body. His decaying jaw hung awkwardly from his skull as he tried to smile. His lightless eyes fixed on me—his prey. Strings of dark gray hair hung from his head like oily weeds.

I wrinkled my nose. "You have obviously been in that stolen corpse for far too long."

The Shadow Lord's jaw flapped as he spoke. "We don't have the luxury of being born in human form like you Watchers." He hissed like a snake.

My foot whipped into his ribs and I heard a sickening crunch.

Adrenaline usually drowned out my body's cries of pain. For that reason, I avoided combat while barefoot—or in a bathrobe, for that matter. The Shadow Lord crumpled from the strike.

My hands sparked with light to finish the job. His bony hands shot toward my throat like ten fingers of lightning.

His pupils narrowed to a slit as more snake-like features emerged. I would never get used to the look in a rebel's eyes before they kill. There's no humanity—only the look of a wild animal driven by carnal appetite.

A stream of flames blasted into his face from my fingers. I didn't hold back. The decaying flesh melted off his skull. His eyes whirled and then dropped from their sockets. I cringed at the rancid smell of burning flesh and held my breath. The corpse hit the ground, and the shadowy spirit of the rebel floated above the scorched remains.

I had seen dozens of dark souls like this one. As much as I wanted to destroy these disembodied Shadows, I couldn't. Blades and fire just passed right through them.

The ghostly form floated toward me. Its movements were slow in its acceptance of temporary defeat, but its unbeatable pride showed through in its burning sulfuric eyes. I held perfectly still as the Shadow leaned over my shoulder and whispered in my ear, "There is nothing you can do. Why keep fighting? In the end, all Watchers and the humans you protect will be destroyed."

I wasn't going to be intimidated. "The smallest flame will stand out in a dark room, but no darkness can survive in the light." An inferno of heat billowed off my shoulders as a visual statement. "As long as there is at least one Watcher on Earth, there is still hope that Erebus will be defeated."

"We shall see." The Shadow's eyes smoldered before he seeped into the floor, leaving me alone in my charred washroom.

Now that I didn't have to hold my tough composure, I dropped my shoulders and wrapped my robe tighter across my chest.

Through my bare window, the night sky glittered with blue stars. I didn't remember Neviah, but every time I looked at the sky, I felt home sick. Being courageous can be very lonely.

I closed my eyes to take in a deep cleansing breath, but coughed out the smell of burnt flesh that still lingered in the room.

For the most part, I kept my powers under control so my clothes didn't burn. I assessed the damaged curtains, burn marks on the walls, and pile of ash on the floor.

"Great." I dropped my hands to my sides. This wasn't going to make anyone in the castle happy. I didn't look forward to begging for forgiveness over another victorious battle.

King Henry had esteemed me as England's Divine Protector. However, after the king's death, his son, Edward, had changed the way the castle was run. Edward saw me as a fashion accessory to have at his side during feasts and celebrations.

"Oh no!" I shouted and clenched my hair in my hands. "The celebration!"

I shut the washroom door behind me and raced down the hallway lined in royal-crested banners to my bedroom where my handmaid waited. No doubt I would be late again. In my mind, I could already see King Edward's look of disapproval. I hated the way he clicked his tongue at me as if I were a child and not a nineteen-year-old lady.

"There you are, Lady Auriella." My handmaid, Eleanor, used a chiding tone that preceded a lecture. "The celebration is about to start, and you're not dressed. We still need to pin up your hair, and you know it takes twice as long to tame those wild, red waves of yours."

I submitted myself to being dressed and primped. Hopefully, I could get on everyone's good side before I confessed my fire slaying deed.

Eleanor escorted me to the vanity and forced me to sit in the chair. I could tell she was in a hurry by the way she pulled on my hair and dug the pins into my scalp. I tried to smile pleasantly and not show any sign of discomfort.

She slowed her pace slightly as she decorated my hair with beads and made sure each lock was in its place.

"Did you fall asleep in the bath-tub?" Eleanor asked.

"No," I answered and cringed at the sound of guilt lacing my voice. From the mirror I watched Eleanor's expression harden.

"Did you get into another fight?" she asked through tight lips. I was sure she already knew the answer.

I dropped my shoulders and nodded.

"Is there ash in the washroom?"

I sank lower in the chair and nodded again.

Eleanor shook her head. "The maids aren't going to be happy with you. What did you destroy this time?"

I bit my lower lip to avoid smiling. "A Shadow Lord." I tried not to sound too sheepish or too proud. After all, it was my duty to protect England from the Shadow Legion.

"Don't speak of such horrible nonsense. There's no such thing. If you didn't have the king's protection, you would have been executed on the grounds of witchcraft for using your fire."

"I'm not a witch," I mumbled under my breath.

The subject aroused anxiety and distain. Witches use their powers for selfish reasons. Watchers use their gifts to protect others.

Eleanor pulled on my hair to make me sit up straight. "Hold still." She didn't hide the irritation in her voice. "I want to know what you destroyed in the washroom. You better not have broken any more mirrors."

"It was a pretty quick fight. At least there's no blood to clean up." I tried to sound positive. After all, I had done a good thing.

"I hope you left the curtains intact."

I swallowed so loud I thought for sure Eleanor heard me. Eleanor frowned. I couldn't hide my guilt.

She finished placing the last few beaded clips into my hair. "I doubt even your abilities can save you from the seamstress's wrath once she finds out about the curtains." Eleanor shook her head. "I swear that woman is part Viking."

I cringed and started strategizing tactics to avoid everyone in the castle, especially the seamstress.

Eleanor didn't look sympathetic. "Now come to the bedpost so I can tighten your corset."

I groaned. My body was already stiff with stress. "How about we skip the corset this time? It's worse than wearing armor on a hot day."

Eleanor let out a fluttery laugh that wasn't meant to be attractive. "Anyone who can wear armor can wear a whale-boned corset."

I raised my eyebrow and challenged, "Anyone?" The thought of the knights of England wearing corsets during training made me giggle. The stress started to melt away as I laughed.

Eleanor laughed with me. "Well, not anyone. We'd have better luck strapping a corset to one of your Shadow Lords before strapping one onto a man."

I gripped the bedpost and laid my head against the wood while Eleanor wrapped the torture device around me and pulled back on the strings. "Now exhale," she said.

When I exhaled, Eleanor cinched the corset tighter, pushing my bust unnaturally high and crushing my ribs. "Not too tight, Eleanor." I intentionally slouched so the corset couldn't be fastened so tightly that it would prevent me from eating the roast and pies I had seen earlier in the kitchen.

Eleanor fought against me and jerked back on the corset laces. "It's time to start dressing and acting like a lady. I know you have duties and all, but you're frightening the suitors."

My hands molded to the shape of bedpost as I squeezed against the pain. "Am I?"

I considered myself a friendly person. Most of the knights and guards I trained with seemed to enjoy my company. I knew there were a few who were interested in courting me, but I usually managed to avoid them. King Edward made it perfectly clear that men only saw my pretty face and feminine shape. No human man would accept me for what I really was.

"You're too intimidating," Eleanor declared. "That's why the lords and knights shy away from you. You're nineteen, still unmarried, and without prospects. You have all the beauty of a queen, but you need to be more vulnerable."

I gasped from more than just the pressure of the corset. "Vulnerable? Tonight in the washroom, I'd never felt more vulnerable in my life. I hadn't noticed the rebel until it was almost too late. I was completely distracted by my day-dream about . . ." I stopped and swallowed hard. I didn't want to bring up my dead fiancé. I still had nightmares about his death.

"So that's the real reason why you've been scaring away the suitors." Eleanor hummed like she'd discovered some deep, dark secret. "It's that boy, the one who was killed on the crusade."

"I guess." My voice dropped to a whisper to hide the surfacing emotions. "I wish I knew what happened to him. All I received was a formal letter saying he had been killed."

I tried to imagine what Lucas would look like if he were still alive. He would be twenty-three now. King Edward had only been a prince at the time he led the crusaders. I would never admit it aloud, but part of me resented that Edward returned, when so many of the men he led had not.

My gaze lowered to nothing in particular. "The crusaders never brought back his body. We didn't even have a memorial because his mother died a few days after we were informed of his death." I glanced at the drawer where I hid my enchanted ruby necklace. If only Lady Hannah had worn it, she would still be alive.

"Poor dear." Eleanor patted my hand. "After all these years, you still haven't found closure. War is a horrible place to be." She shook her head. "But the wives who suddenly become widows, the children who become fatherless, and the sweethearts who will never love again are the real victims."

I blinked several times to force back tears. Her words stabbed my soul. Was I really doomed to never love again?

Eleanor faced me. "You can't keep looking behind you, Auriella. You need to set your sights straight ahead of you. It's been years since Lucas died. It's time to move on."

The corset prevented me from taking a deep breath. I looked out the balcony doors at the night sky instead. Perhaps it was true that I was creating my own tragedy by refusing to move on, but I wasn't sure I really could move on. Maybe I believed that no one would ever love me as much as Lucas. Maybe I was afraid of betraying the deceased since I still felt loyalty to him.

"Now, which dress should you wear?" Eleanor pulled open the wardrobe doors and laid several dresses on the bed.

"The indigo and silver one." I pointed to the last dress King Henry gave me before he died.

"Are you sure? This dress makes your hair look even redder."

I put my hands on my hips and tried not to laugh at Eleanor's serious, yet ridiculous, statement. "There's nothing wrong with having red hair."

Eleanor shook her head. "People will think you have a temper."

I gave her a mock scowl.

"Very well," Eleanor surrendered. She tossed the dress over my head and laced up the back. I adjusted the cloth and strapped my sword to my side.

Eleanor's fingers strained as if she wanted to snatch the sword away from me. She probably would have if she had not been afraid to touch a weapon. "You cannot take a sword to the celebration. No man will ask you to dance."

"I know you think I am scaring them off, but I'm just filtering out the suitors who lack courage," I said and really meant it.

"At least you'd be filtering out the sober ones," Eleanor mumbled. "You have a lot to learn about men, Lady Auriella. You are never going to find a proper husband while you carry a weapon."

The doors swung open. "Ah, there you are." King Edward held out his arms and gave me a broad, false smile. Someday that man was going to learn to knock before entering a woman's chamber. He needed a lesson in chivalry as much as the Rebellion did.

Eleanor and I both curtsied to the king.

"You look splendid, Lady Auriella." I mechanically held up my hand, and King Edward kissed the top of it. "My lady, I have magnificent news for you. I have filled the position of the captain of the guard."

"That's wonderful," I said, but I really wanted to say, "Finally!" The position had been vacant for several years, ever since I exposed the former captain as a Shadow Legionnaire. After Prince Edward took the throne, finding a new captain for castle security hadn't been his priority. He focused on battles in the surrounding countries. His dream was to see all the Britannia Isles, including Scotland and Ireland, united under his rule.

"The new captain arrives tonight," Edward said. "I'm sure he will want to meet with you, if he's not busy with more important matters." I tried not to look insulted at Edward's suggestion that it wouldn't be important for the new captain to meet with me, the warrior who had protected the castle for the last few years.

Edward continued, "I told him you are a Watcher who guards us from all things unholy." He lifted his nose. "The new captain is not a superstitious man. He wants to make sure you are legitimate."

"What does that mean?" I tried to keep my voice lady-like and gentle, though my eyes narrowed.

"He asked if I had ever seen a member of the Shadow Legion, and I told him no. He thinks you might be a fraud."

"What?" I almost shouted. "I killed a Legionnaire less than an hour ago. They are real. You haven't seen any because I'm doing my job."

"My lady." King Edward took my hand and patted it. "I'm not going to dismiss you. I would much rather see you married to one of my deserving military leaders."

I clenched my teeth and slammed all the doors to my heart shut. I was not a reward for the king to give. I pulled away and crossed my arms.

Edward looked around the room. "Where is that lovely dress I just got you?"

"It's with the seamstress for adjustments," I explained. "The dress was too low-cut for my taste."

"But not for others' tastes." Edward smoothed out his mustache and turned to Eleanor. "Fetch the scarlet dress from the seamstress."

"Wait." I thought quickly. I didn't want to wear something that would reiterate the king's beliefs that I was just an object of visual pleasure. "I want to wear this dress." I motioned toward the one I wore. "It was the last gift your father gave me. I want to honor him by wearing it to the celebration of your latest victory over the Scottish."

King Edward smiled. "It was one of my greatest victories. You will see, Lady Auriella, this war is in everyone's best interest. When the French or Spanish grow restless, England acts as a shield for Scotland and Ireland. It's best we unite these countries under our flag if we are going to protect them."

I nodded. Thankfully I had distracted him from forcing me to wear something that would make me feel uncomfortable.

"We are even providing them with modern medicine and education. I don't know why the Scottish and Irish barbarians keep fighting us."

The king shrugged, and then ran his hand over my cheek. My body went rigid under the gesture. "Don't worry about the barbarians, m'lady. You have more pressing matters, like enjoying the festivities of tonight." The king kissed my hand then headed toward the door as if he was leaving. A wicked smile curled his lips. "One more thing," he said catching my attention. "Leave the sword behind." His jaw hardened, as did his icy voice. "That is an order from your king." He slammed the door behind him.

Chapter Two

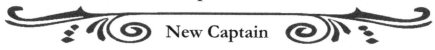

New Captain

I gripped the belt that held the sword to my waist. If I didn't know better, by the way King Edward tried to stop me from doing my job, I would think he worked for the Shadow Legion. I had the distinct feeling he wanted to eliminate my position as England's Watcher. No matter how many times I explained to him in confidence that I was not a human, he still saw me as just a woman, and women in this society did not hold protective positions.

I unbuckled my belt and dropped the sword on my bed. I refused to be defeated so easily.

"It's best to follow orders," Eleanor reminded. She cringed at the sword as if it were a cockroach lying on my pillow.

I ignored her and dug through the mahogany chest at the foot of my bed. A Watcher had to be ready at any moment for a fight, but I would also have to be discreet to appease everyone. I found a brass-handled dagger under several quilts in the chest and unsheathed it.

"My lady?" Eleanor gasped. Horror washed over her face. I tried not to laugh at her overreaction.

I lightly touched the blade to make sure it was sharp. "If I let down my guard for one moment, I could be killed. I'm not an Immortal you know," I said in my most serious tone, hoping Eleanor wouldn't try to stop me.

She wrung her hands. "But the king said—"

I cut her off before she got too worked up. "As a Watcher, my orders come from the King of Neviah. Besides, King Edward said, 'no swords.'" I held up the dagger and winked. "This is not a sword. No one will even know I have it." I hiked up my skirt, exposing my legs. "Hand me some hair ribbons."

She shook her head and reluctantly handed me the ribbons from the vanity drawer. "I have a feeling we are both going to get into trouble for this."

I tied the weapon to my leg, smoothed out my dress, and then clasped the ruby necklace around my neck. "There. Now I'm ready to go." I felt like a warrior in disguise and loved the devious energy rushing through me. Having a weapon always made me feel more confident, especially when my energy was low.

Eleanor crossed her arms and assessed me. Despite her opposition to what I was hiding under, she seemed to approve of my lady-like appearance. "You'd better hurry. You're already late."

I sprinted down the hallway to the ballroom. The train of my dress whipped behind like a ship's flag in a storm. As I approached the ballroom, I slid my back against the wall and peered around the corner. The doors were already closed, which meant everyone was sure to notice my entrance. I smiled and tried not to look suspicious as I glided toward the ballroom. Two doormen bowed and opened the double doors wide, exposing me to the hundreds of people inside.

Laughter and music from the ball echoed throughout the room and hit me with warmth. Torches blazed on the stone walls, and the red and gold flag of England hung over the banister. Lords and ladies danced methodically around the great hall. Flavorful scents of perfume and of the prepared feast washed over me.

There was only one problem. "A masquerade ball." I slapped my hand over my forehead. If I had gotten a formal invitation with the details instead of just being expected to show up, I would have known I needed a mask. There had to be something I could use for a mask. I looked around the hall and yanked a laced doily out from under a vase and put it on my head.

I made my way along the edges of the ballroom and discreetly took my place two seats from King Edward. My fingers trembled as I fussed with my layered indigo and silver gown. I tried not to make eye contact with the king, hoping he hadn't noticed my entrance.

"Ah! Lady Auriella!" My whole body tensed and my teeth snapped together when I heard his boisterous voice. "Delayed by demons again, were we?" He wasted no time with his mockery. Edward and the other men at the table laughed and threw me sardonic glances.

I ignored them and focused on the plate of food in front of me. I didn't want to cause more of a scene than Edward already had. Hopefully he'd go back to his drunken conversation.

"Lady Auriella, is that a doily on your head?" he asked.

I pulled it off my head, causing a few of the beads Eleanor had meticulously placed in my hair to be flung to the ground and roll under the table. This night was already a disaster.

King Edward leaned over the man sitting next to him and gripped my knee.

I jumped and put my hand protectively over the dagger.

"Nervous?" he asked with a crooked smile.

I searched his eyes for hidden meaning. Did I look as subordinate as I felt? I didn't exhale until King Edward released his grip on me. I turned my gaze to the lords and ladies dancing around the room, but I could still feel the king's eyes on me. I had to distract him from his scrutinizing assessment. "Congratulations on your victory over the Scottish," I said without looking at him. Distraction by flattery always worked with Edward.

From the corner of my eye, I saw Edward lean back and relax. "Our kingdom's military is strong. We are undoubtedly a world power. Not even Erebus and his Shadow Legion could defeat us." Mockery laced his tone and invited the other men to laugh at me.

The statement was a direct assault at undermining my position again. Despite his cruelty, I forced myself to smile pleasantly. "Erebus is a master tactician," I reminded. "There is no kingdom on this planet immune to the dark powers of his Shadow Legion." My lips lifted in one corner, and I looked into his eyes, trying to pierce trepidation into him. "If your kingdom is so well protected, perhaps I should move on and find another that needs me." It was the best I could do at threatening him without losing my life or being banished.

"I'd rather see you married than leave the country and become a traitor." King Edward laughed politely, but his teeth snapped together when his jaw flexed.

I pretended to be shocked by his comment. "No, Your Highness, I wouldn't dream of leaving the country if you still need my protection." I put my hand to my heart and batted my eyelashes innocently.

King Edward laughed and pounded his fist against the table, making the dishes rattle. The guests at the table held their wine goblets to keep the liquid from spilling. "My lady," Edward said, "Look! I have all these strong men to protect me." He motioned to the captains on his right and left. "I'm sure they can handle anything a Watcher could face."

"And there's the new captain of the guard," one of the men added.

"That's right," the king said. "He should be here any moment." He took a sip from his goblet and changed the subject. "Any suitors come to call, Lady Auriella? You're twenty-three now, right?"

"Nineteen," I corrected. Angry heat rose to my face. "I guess I'm doomed to be an old maid because I'm too intimidating," I quoted Eleanor and tried to sound like I didn't care.

The king shook his head and waved his hand. "Nonsense, you're fragile and vulnerable just like any other female."

I furrowed my brow. Did Edward not remember I was one of the best warriors in England? I could make fire come from my hands and owned a necklace that could heal me while I fought. I touched the ruby in the gold and silver pendant of my necklace. I turned away and pushed back the pain swelling in my heart. I had to focus on something else before I started feeling sorry for myself. I picked up a spoon and pushed at the food on my plate. Maybe if I didn't look and act so human, the king would respect me. I looked down at the rainbow ring glistened on my finger.

The king gulped down his wine and slammed the empty goblet onto the table. "I'm sure there are more productive things a woman like you could do instead of chasing phantoms."

He wasn't going to let this go. He was intentionally trying to aggravate me. I shook my head. "The Shadow Legionnaires are real."

King Edward was only partially paying attention to me as he listened in on another conversation down the table. "Yes, yes, another pile of ash, I presume." He turned to the other discussion and made a remark.

I broke my perfect posture and leaned as far back in the chair as my corset would allow. Things had been much easier when King Henry was alive. He fully supported my position as England's Watcher, while King Edward treated me like a nuisance. He never cared to hear any of my reports or take precautions to protect the castle against the Shadow Legion.

The king turned back to me and I prepared for another verbal beating. "Lady Auriella, would you mind saving a dance for the new captain of the guard?" His eyes wavered with drunkenness.

My jaw tightened, but I forced myself to sound polite. "Unfortunately, Your Majesty, I will be retiring early tonight." Before he could argue, I stood from the table and marched through the crowd of nobles toward the exit. I didn't need to be harassed like this, not even by an ignorant king.

It didn't matter how strong England's armies were. Humans could not stand on their own against the Shadow Legion. Erebus wanted Earth for himself, and the only way to achieve his goal was through the complete genocide of the human race. I pressed my lips into a thin line and sped toward the exit.

I didn't feel bad about leaving early. I had made my appearance, been the source of rude entertainment for the king and his captains, and then left.

Even with the late hour, the castle seemed eerily quiet. I rushed down the vacant hall toward my room. The windows let in streams of silver moonlight and broke up the pitch dark hallway.

I dropped my hand to my side. The metal of the dagger pressed against my warm thigh. I entered my quiet room and shut the doors to drown out the sound of the war celebration. King Edward would be disappointed that I didn't dance or even meet with his new captain of the guard.

The new captain had already accused me of being a fraud. Our relationship wasn't going to be pleasant. I was glad I got out of there before I was forced to dance with him. My pained reflection in the mirror stared back at me. My earrings clinked when I dropped them in a porcelain dish next to the mirror. I had duties, and my duties always came before pleasure. I pulled the pins from my hair, letting the locks fall around my face.

I replaced my elaborate dress with a simple linen night gown and wandered onto the balcony. London glinted with lamplights, like the sea of stars above. The cold night air whipped through my hair and clothes, bathing me in a refreshing storm. It was selfish of me to desire more than what I had been given. It's a flawed human trait to want what you can't have and not appreciate what you do have. I slouched pathetically against the railing and touched my ruby necklace. If the feelings of love, loss, guilt, and helplessness were so human then why was I feeling this way?

I let out a deep sigh and looked at the night sky. Somewhere, on a planet near the North Star, the war against Erebus and his Legion started. We would finish the battle here on Earth.

I turned to my room and noticed an ivory parchment on the dresser next to my mirror. It was marked with a seal. At first, I thought it was King Edward's seal. Of course, he never sent me letters or invitations. A crossed rose and arrow embossed the red wax seal. This wasn't from Edward.

I carefully broke the seal and read:

Aura, London is Erebus's next target. Help is on the way.

I looked around my room. Who had sent this? What did they mean by help is on the way? How did they know this?

The lamps in the room extinguished, darkness flooded my chambers, and the air went bitterly cold. I dropped the letter.

"Erebus," I whispered. He was already here?

I lifted the skirt of my nightgown and slid the dagger strapped to my leg from the scabbard.

A figure stood ominously in the moonlight streaming through the balcony.

"Show yourself!" I demanded and then whispered to myself, "Oh, please don't be a Shadow Wolf."

The room illuminated as a flame burst to life. I squinted as the small flicker of light touched the top of an oil-soaked lamp wick.

My eyes adjusted to the sudden brightness.

As soon as I made eye contact with him, I collapsed to the ground. How could this be? All strength in my body dispersed. The dagger fell from my grip. It couldn't be him. I covered my mouth with a quivering hand and gasped for air. This wasn't possible.

I lifted my head and met his gaze. "Lucas?" I hadn't spoken his name since he died, yet it fell from my lips with surprising grace. "Lucas? How —"

Lucas rushed forward and knelt on the floor beside me. I reached for him, but stopped, afraid my hand would pass through the phantom of my past. Lucas must have sensed my hesitation. He reached out and caressed my face. I leaned into his touch—solid and gentle. Calluses from the years of hard work in the stables still marked his strong, familiar hands.

As I had done hundreds of times before, I reached up and pushed back the stubborn lock of hair that always hung in his face. His jaw was firmer than I remembered, but it was him. His shoulders and chest had broadened over the years, and he was stronger, much stronger.

"Surprise," Lucas whispered. He gave a soft, low laugh. "I'm sorry, I didn't mean to scare you. I just saw your balcony doors open and –"

"How did you climb up here?" I didn't wait for him to answer. I knew. It was the same way we always snuck out to be together when we lived at the manor in Oswestry.

All my tension melted away, but elation, disbelief, and confusion swirled inside me. Lucas helped me to my feet and held me close.

I stammered, trying to explain, "The crusades . . . we got a letter." My thoughts and emotions ran together as I realized my fiancé was back from the dead.

"My lady, Auriella." His voice echoed in my mind, pulling buried emotions to the surface. "You are still so beautiful, just as I remember." Lucas's cold hands wrapped around my waist and pulled me close.

"You are freezing." I hurried to the balcony doors and shut them. I held his hand to my lips and blew warm air on his fingers.

"Where have you been?" Liquid pain burned in my eyes and streamed down my cheeks. "Why didn't you come for me sooner?" My legs shook as I leaned against him.

"I am here now," Lucas said, with an apologetic smile. "It wasn't easy finding you." He kissed my hands, making me shiver. "I promised I would return for you. You can always trust me to keep my promises."

Happy memories flooded over me. He was my best friend, and I shared all my secrets with him—every secret, but one. I had never told him about my ethereal heritage or powers, and I regretted it.

Looking back and seeing him here now, I knew Lucas would love me no matter who or what I was.

"Lucas." I took his hands. "I have something I need to tell you." I sat on the bed, and tried to stream my swimming thoughts into elegant words.

"What is it?" Concern washed over his face as he sat next to me. He had a look that said, "You can tell me anything."

I furrowed my brow. "Have you talked with Alwaien?" I thought for sure Lucas would have returned to Oswestry first. That's where he left me, and that's where he promised to return.

"Alwaien?" Lucas looked confused.

Now I was confused. "Your brother?" I prodded.

Lucas lifted his hand to his head. "I was injured. Some of my memories aren't as clear any more, but I have seen you in my dreams every night since I left and have thought of nothing more than returning for you."

"I thought about you every day too," I said and reached for his hand. So much had changed since then, but the truth about what had happened after he left crushed down on me. I keep my voice soft and sympathetic. "Lucas, I'm not the Lady of Oswestry anymore. I gave up my inheritance and title."

I held my breath and waited for his response.

"Why?" He blinked several times.

"I couldn't stay there anymore. I left after your mother died." I bit my lip and braced myself to see the man I loved in pain.

There was a moment of silence that seemed to last forever. "She's dead?" Lucas lowered his head and pressed his fingers over his eyes.

His body quivered. "How did she die?"

I touched the delicate pendant of the ruby necklace that hung around my neck like a heavy chain of guilt. It could have healed her if she would have just worn it. "She died of a broken heart," I said. "And I thought my fate would be the same."

His hands pressed against my back in a painful embrace as he sobbed. I held my breath as he released his anguish. "What happened after she died?"

I tightened my jaw and wondered how much emotional heartache Lucas could take in one night. "I left Oswestry and, now, I'm working in the castle."

"As a servant?" Lucas let me go. His eyes widened with horror. "Why would you lower yourself to such a state? I will take you away from here. You, my lady, deserve your rightful status of a noble woman."

"No, it's not like that," I assured. "I'm the kingdom's Watcher." I knew the title would open a floodgate of questions. Lucas held perfectly still. I couldn't read his emotions, so I immediately started apologizing. "I'm so sorry I kept this secret from you. I thought you wouldn't love me if you knew I had powers. If . . . I wasn't normal." I took a deep breath and whispered, "I'm not human."

"You're a Neviahan?" His lips formed a smirk. "A super-being from fairy-tales?"

I clasped my hands together, pleading for forgiveness. "I'm so sorry." I waited for him to recoil from me like a plague.

The lamplight glinted off the tears I desperately tried to hold back. I blinked the liquid away to clear my vision. Lucas would probably hate me, or at least fear me. Perhaps I made a mistake by confessing my heritage.

Lucas's expression changed from disbelief to confusion before he smiled at me and clutched my hands "My lady, it doesn't matter what you are. You are just as human to me as anyone else."

I released my tight breath and dropped my shoulders, letting the tension go. "Really? You still love me?"

Lucas nodded. "Of course."

I held his hand and pressed the back of it to my face in adoration. "Where have you been this whole time?"

Lucas shrugged away from me, and I immediately felt guilty for asking. "I was crusading with Prince Edward, now King Edward. We were attacked, and I was left for dead."

"Lucas, no. That's why it took you so long to return." I put my hands to my mouth to muffle my gasp. It was just like Edward to leave men behind and save himself.

"But I never forgot about my vow to marry you when I returned." Lucas opened his hand. A gold ring with eight laurel leaves engraved in the metal glistened off his palm.

I stopped breathing as he slipped off the bed and knelt on the floor next to me.

"Lucas?" My heart raced and my hand quivered in his. I once again wondered if I was dreaming this surreal moment.

"While I was in Rome, I told myself I would give this to you when I asked if you still wanted to marry me." He placed the ring in my hand.

I ran my finger along the smooth edge of the gold band and swallowed. It was a miracle Lucas was back from the dead. I now had closure from the war, but we had been apart for so long and much had changed. Even though he had returned from war, my war against the Shadow Legion wouldn't end any time soon. If he married me, he would still be in danger and targeted by the Shadows who hunted me.

I hadn't looked up from the ring on my palm. I could only imagine the turmoil my silence caused Lucas. I didn't know what to say to him. I did love him and I remembered wanting nothing more than to be his wife. Why was I questioning this decision? Lucas had been through so much to return to me. I looked up at him. His face was white with horror as he obviously sensed my inner struggle.

I had to say something. I had to say "yes." I owed it to him.

Before I could say anything the handle to my door clicked. King Edward burst into the room with a wide grin. "I'm not interrupting anything am I?"

I groaned inwardly at Edward's invasion and twisted my lips in disgust. I hoped he could tell I was livid at him for destroying this private moment. I realized I was wearing my nightgown, which only intensified my embarrassment and anger. I pulled away from Lucas and threw a robe around my nightgown.

Edward seemed too pleased.

Lucas got off his knee and bowed to the king.

"Ah," the king said stroking his beard. "Auriella, I see you have met the new captain of the guard?"

I furrowed my brow. "New captain of the guard?"

"I was going to surprise you at the dance," Lucas said. "But you didn't wait for me. Edward said you ran off with some other man so I went to retrieve for you."

Some other man? The situation was becoming more complicated by the minute. I couldn't help but blame Edward for that. "There was no other man."

King Edward flipped his hand, making all the rings on his fingers sparkle. "Now that you two have officially met, I'm requesting that you join me in the war room tomorrow morning. There are a few security concerns I want to address with the both of you."

"We will be there," Lucas said resolutely.

I searched Lucas's face for answers, but confusion still overwhelmed me. "Wait." I held up my hands and turned to Lucas. "You're the new captain of the guard?" The information slowly settled in my mind.

"Of course he is," King Edward said. "Didn't he tell you?"

I cast a sideways glance at Lucas. "I'm sure he was going to tell me, but we were interrupted." I meant it as a sarcastic insinuation, but Edward didn't seem to take the hint.

"Yes." King Edward leaned back and pulled up on his gemmed belt. "Lucas and I met on the crusades."

I bit my tongue to keep from saying, "And you left him for dead."

"He will make a great captain of the guard."

"Yes he will," I finally agreed on something with Edward. I loved that Lucas and I would be in charge of protecting the castle together. "I would like to inform Lucas about a few things before our meeting tomorrow," I said and gave Lucas's hand three quick squeezes as an indication that we needed to get rid of Edward so we could speak privately. Since Lucas was the new captain of the guard, I should tell him about the strange letter I received regarding Erebus's plans to attack.

"Yes." Lucas took the hint and played along. "We were about to discuss castle security."

"In Auriella's private chamber?" King Edward raised an eyebrow and nodded toward our interlocked hands.

Lucas dropped my hand. "We can discuss this in detail at our meeting tomorrow." He turned the king around and motioned toward the door. "I'm sure you have some splendid strategies you want us to implement." Lucas looked over his shoulder and winked at me as he escorted the king out of my chamber.

Lucas would always be my hero. I slipped the engagement ring on my finger. I would never lose him again.

Chapter Three

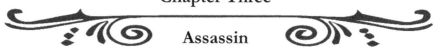

Assassin

It was still dark the next morning when I met Lucas in the hallway just outside the war room. His arms slipped around my back in a gentle embrace.

"Are you nervous?" he asked and kissed me lightly on the cheek. He was in a better mood than I was.

"Of course I'm nervous." I pulled away from him and refused comfort. "I heard a rumor that the king wants to give me a new assignment. I'm a Watcher, and my duty is to protect humans from the Shadow Legion." I took a deep breath and looked away so Lucas wouldn't see my irritated expression. Why wouldn't the king just let me do my job?

Lucas pursed his lips. "I don't know what your new assignment will be, but we will work together, as a team. There's nothing you and I can't do." His hands clasped around mine, and his eyes went wild with excitement. "We could conquer the whole world together."

I couldn't help but smile. "You said the same thing to me years ago when we were only children." I had missed his enthusiasm. He stepped in for a kiss, but I turned away and nervously twisted the ring around my finger. "Last night I received some information about the Legion."

"The Legion?" Curiosity laced his voice.

"Yes." I pulled away and paced in front of the heavy doors of the war room. "I have reason to believe the Shadow Legion will soon launch a major invasion on London."

Lucas gripped my hand to keep me from pacing. "I don't think they will come to London," he assured. "Why would they invade when you're here to protect the castle?"

I smiled. At least Lucas appreciated my position.

Lucas shrugged. "What's so bad about the Shadow Legion, anyway?"

His question reminded me how human he was. Not many humans knew about Watchers or the Shadow Legion. I glanced around the hall to be sure no one else could hear us. "The Shadow Legionnaires kill humans, and then steal their bodies." I leaned closer and whispered, "They disguise themselves in human flesh."

Lucas raised one eyebrow. "So the shadow just slips inside the body like a glove and animates it?"

My muscles tightened at the gory description. He said it with such naiveté that it made me shiver. He was like a little child facing monsters in an otherworldly war. "Yes," I said. "Not only that, but they can possess living beings as well."

"Wouldn't it be too crowded with two souls in one body?" Lucas asked.

I nodded and started pacing again. "With living beings, the Shadow Spirits have a harder time controlling the host. That's why they prefer dead humans. Sometimes the Shadow will try to convince the host to kill himself so it can take full control of the body."

Lucas crossed his arms. "Sounds disgusting."

"It is." I paced faster. I normally didn't talk to people about this, but Lucas would have to be educated if he was going to fight them with me. "Once the Shadow Spirit has a body, it becomes a Shadow Lord. I see at least one a week in this castle. I swear they're after the king. Just think of the damage they could do to the country if they had the king's body and identity."

"Have you warned the king?" Lucas asked.

"A thousand times." I dropped my arms to my sides in defeat. "He just pats my hand and tells me to run along." I imitated Edward by flipping my hand through the air. "What I'm really worried about is Erebus, the Shadow King."

Lucas leaned forward, his eyes wide. "Shadow King?"

It was refreshing to talk with someone who actually took an interest in my work instead of acting as if I was trying to scare people with ghost stories.

"Erebus and his Legion crave power, which is why they crave Neviahan blood. If they drink my blood, they will steal my powers."

Lucas gripped my shoulder to stop me from pacing again. "Shouldn't we be protecting you then?" A smile curled on his lips.

"I'm not afraid of the Legionnaires." I looked away and admitted, "But I'm not sure if I could defeat the Shadow King. Last night I got a message that Erebus plans to invade London." I swallowed hard.

"What? Who?" Lucas's eyes went wide. His expression seemed to contain a mix of fear and hate.

I looked at him, surprised by his abrupt change in mood. "Erebus," I repeated. Why was Lucas acting this way?

Lucas shook his head. "No, not him. Who told you about Erebus?"

Now I was confused. I furrowed my brow and answered, "I only got a letter saying that Erebus was coming, but help is on the way. You and I may need to hold Erebus off until that help arrives."

Lucas leaned back and clenched his hair in his fists. "Was the messenger a Watcher, like you?" His words were filled with revulsion.

"I don't know. It was just a letter." I crossed my arms and refused to answer any more questions until he calmed down and told me why he was so irritated.

"It's probably a Watcher from a nearby kingdom." Lucas's voice rose in volume. "What else did the letter say? Did it say who would be with him?"

I shook my head. "What is wrong?" I hoped his anger wasn't a prejudice against Watchers. "Why are you so upset? We can at least prepare for an attack."

Lucas closed his eyes and took several deep breaths.

"Lucas," I said clearly, "you're not the same boy I knew." I tried not to sound offended by him. "I've never seen you lose your temper."

He opened his eyes and regained his calm composure. "War changes people, Auriella. You're right, I'm not the same boy you loved. I'm a powerful man now." Lucas looked away. "Tell me all you know about the upcoming invasion and what you've done to protect the castle," he prodded.

"Nothing yet," I admitted. "I only learned about the invasion last night. That's why I need your help, Lucas." I put my hand over his.

Lucas looked down and stared at my finger. "You're wearing it." He traced the engagement ring.

I relaxed and smiled back at him. "It's a perfect fit."

He pressed my hand to his lips. "A perfect fit, just like us." He paused then added, "I hoped just you and I would fight Erebus, without the Watchers' help."

I raised one eyebrow. "Are you sure this isn't your masculine pride getting in the way?"

"Not at all, my lady. Think of it as proof of my love for you."

Before I could explain he didn't need to prove anything, two guards opened the doors to the king's war room.

"Come in," King Edward beckoned.

I regally straightened my shoulders and reminded myself that, despite my romantic relationship with Lucas, I was England's Watcher and had to represent my position well in front of the king.

As we entered I noted a map draped over a massive square table in the center of the room. A silver tray of food sat on top of the map in front of King Edward. Lucas and I waited as Edward continued to eat then lick the last bit of flavor from his fingers.

I met Lucas's gaze. His eyes were alight with the curiosity I felt. "Your Majesty," Lucas started, breaking the silence. "About Auriella's assignment—"

"Oh, yes," the king said. He wiped his lips on a linen napkin. "As you know, the country's greatest threat is from the north."

Edward set the napkin on the map and pointed to the country of Scotland.

"Yes," Lucas said. "The Scottish barbarians."

I didn't agree with them. Our country's greatest threat was the Shadow Legion. Erebus was going to attack any day, but there was no use in voicing my opinion to Edward. I held my tongue to see where the king was going with his speculation and what he thought I could do about it.

"I do not want war," King Edward said in a righteous tone. "I want to see all of Britannia united under one flag." He pointed to the butter-stained map under his tray of food. "Just think how much stronger we will be if we expand our borders." His tone turned sour. "The Scottish, however, have their own ideas. They want to remain a separate country, which is easy for them since England acts as a buffer from foreign threats." He pointed to England on the map in between Scotland and the rest of the European countries.

"If we are protecting them then we should be taxing them to support our military," Lucas said.

"We are." The king seemed to grow more aggravated. "But now they are refusing to pay taxes."

"Have you tried talking to them?" I asked, but meant it more as a diplomatic suggestion.

King Edward scowled as if I had offended him and his leadership abilities. Then his face softened, and he gave me an amused smile. "It's just like a woman to suggest such a thing."

The statement felt like a slap in the face, and I was sure he meant it that way.

Lucas continued to look at the map. "How can we make the Scottish respect what England does for them?"

"We have no choice but war." Edward turned and hovered over the map with Lucas. They had their backs to me as if intentionally blocking me out of the conversation. "They are building up a military force against us here, here, and here." Edward pointed to a few places on the map.

I tried to look over their shoulders at the map. "Why are they building a military force against us?" I asked. "What have we done to them?"

The king slammed his cup on the table. The wine sprayed across the map like red blood. "Nothing," he sputtered. "We have done nothing but protect them, and now they want to attack us."

Lucas leaned back against the table and crossed his arms. "Action needs to be taken to protect ourselves and recover lost taxes, but why have you called Lady Auriella to this meeting? What has she got to do with the Scottish?" he asked, cutting to the chase. "She is the Watcher, and her place is with me." He stopped, cleared his throat, and restated more formally, "As the captain of the guard, I am in charge of castle security, which would place Auriella under my command."

King Edward took another drink, then lowered his cup. "I'm reassigning her away from the castle."

"What?" Lucas and I said together. The king couldn't dismiss me from my life's calling so easily. The worst I expected him to do was assign me some menial task in the castle to keep me out of his business. But, if he sent me away, the kingdom would be vulnerable to a massive Shadow raid.

Lucas defiantly crossed his arms in front of his chest. I hoped he would say something, anything that would change the king's mind.

"Don't worry." Edward held up his hands. "I'm not sending her away for long."

I mouthed the words "send me away." I hadn't seen Lucas in years and the king wanted me to leave on some obtuse assignment? Edward had horrible timing.

"The last assassins I sent into Scotland never came back." King Edward shook his head. "This time, I need to send in someone the Scots won't suspect." He nodded toward me and winked flirtatiously.

Abhorrence and disbelief struck me. Did he really ask me to do what I thought he did?

"No," Lucas almost shouted. "What if those barbarians catch her?"

The king shrugged. "If they catch her, Auriella will just escape using her fire. She's been very good at starting fires lately."

I cringed and thought about the curtains and tapestries I recently destroyed.

The king leaned forward. His lips curled into a devilish smile. "I need an assassin who can seduce the King of Scots and bring back his head in a bag."

"I can't." I gasped. My whole body trembled like a fragile leaf. I stepped back and bumped into a table. "I'm not supposed to kill humans. My quarrel is with the Rebellion." I'm sure my expression betrayed my terror at the thought of committing such a horrible act. I didn't try to hide how I felt.

"Are you part of this kingdom or not?" King Edward snapped unmercifully.

I tightened my fists and nodded.

Edward pointed his butter-stained fingers at my face. "Then you will do what I order you to do." Saliva spat from his mouth. His face turned red and the tendons in his neck strained under his rage.

Like a damsel in distress, I looked at Lucas, hoping he would save me. He just stood there and stared at the map in deep thought.

Edward lowered his hand. "Now, leave quickly, Lady Auriella. We will celebrate the Scottish king's death when you return."

Lucas and I left the room together, but I refused to hold his hand. Why hadn't he intervened? I didn't say anything to him until we reach the privacy of my room. "Lucas, I can't do it. I can't kill a human." I crossed my arms and leaned against the balcony doors in my bedroom.

Lucas walked toward me. "You have to, Auriella. If you don't, the king will hang you as a traitor."

I took several deep breaths and wiped my face on my sleeve.

"Don't cry, Auriella." Lucas sympathetically wrapped his arms around my waist. "King Edward is right. No one will suspect you, and if you get into trouble, just use your Watcher powers to escape."

"Lucas," I started, searching for a way to help him understand. "Do you remember the shepherds in Oswestry?"

Lucas nodded.

"Think of the King of Neviah as the shepherd. He is good and kind and protects the sheep from the wolves. Humans are sheep and the Shadow Legionnaires are the wolves. The Shadow Legionnaires are humanity's predators. The Shadows will try to destroy and consume everyone on this planet.

"Besides the sheep, there is another member of the flock—the sheepdogs. They are the watchers and guardians of the shepherd's flock."

Lucas's eyes lit up with understanding. "So you're part of the flock and listen to the shepherd's commands even though you are just as dangerous as the wolves."

"Yes," I continued, "My duty is to protect humans and obey the King of Neviah, not the king of England." I opened my balcony doors and stepped outside. Sunlight hit my skin and made me sparkle like an opal chandelier. "Lucas," I breathed. "You see. I'm not human, and I don't get involved with human wars unless the Rebellion is behind it." I stood there, glittering in the sun to prove my point, until I remembered humans couldn't see my beautiful, but strange, mark.

Lucas stepped away from the light. "How do you know the Rebellion isn't behind the Scottish uprising?"

It was a good point. If London was the Legion's next target, the rebels could already have control over the other parts of the islands. I shook my head. "It's not my territory to protect. My job is to guard the humans in England."

"But the king said—" Lucas started.

"I don't take orders from sheep," I said, referring to King Edward.

"Just go to Scotland, Auriella. Take poison, daggers, whatever weapons you need. If the Scottish king is a Shadow Lord, you can kill him without regret." I crossed my arms as Lucas continued. "If the Scottish king is human and all is well, then return and give King Edward whatever information about their country you find. Maybe he will be pleased with the inside information and celebrate your return anyway."

"What about Erebus?" I asked. "We can't forget that he could invade at any moment." I left the balcony and stepped back inside my room.

Lucas closed the doors, making the room dark. "Let me worry about him."

"No, Lucas. You can't fight him alone, and I'm not going to leave you when I know he is near."

Lucas tightened his jaw and I realized I had insulted him. "I thought your little messenger friend said help was on the way."

I dropped my shoulders. It could have been a joke for all I know. I didn't have any details about Erebus's invasion plans, when help would arrive, or who wrote the letter.

Lucas took my hand. "Besides, you need to get away from the castle. You and the king have had too many disagreements. Think of it as a holiday." He smiled pleasantly.

I lowered my gaze to the floor. "I guess it wouldn't hurt to see if Erebus has control of the Scottish monarchy."

Lucas reached into his tunic and pulled out a bottle of black liquid. "If things go bad, use this poison."

"What?" I gasped and covered my mouth. Since when did my sweet Lucas carry poison?

Lucas chuckled. "You're a little jumpy for an assassin."

"Do you always carry poison these days?" I asked.

"I was saving it for something, but now I don't need it. Don't be afraid to use it," he encouraged.

"*If* I use it," I reminded. "I won't hurt a human. I will only use it if the Scottish king is a Shadow Lord."

"Of course," Lucas said. He kissed my forehead and slid the poison into my palm. I stared at the black liquid in my trembling hand. Lucas smiled that boyish smile I cherished. All my past feelings resurfaced as I remembered our friendship and why I loved him.

"I have something for you as well." I unfastened the ruby necklace I always wore.

Lucas's eyes widened.

"This necklace heals your body instantly," I explained. "If I have to leave you alone to fight the Shadow Legionnaires, I want you to have it. I can't lose you again."

Lucas bowed so I could wrap it around his neck and connect the clasp. He examined the jewel. "When you get back, things will be different," he cautioned.

I raised one eyebrow. "Different how?"

His lips lifted into an easy smile as he pointed to the ring on my hand. "I will make you my queen."

Chapter Four

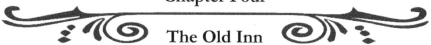

The Old Inn

I looked up at the sky overhead and singled out the North Star. My people called it Kolob, our sun. My hands gripped the reins tighter as the cold night air blew through my hair. I urged my horse forward, quickening the pace. I didn't like being in the woods at night.

The absence of Earth's sun always made me tired. I was starting to think sunlight had something to do with my energy levels. I glanced up at the North Star again and imagined how the light of my home planet's sun would feel like. I took a deep breath, trying to absorb the heat from across the galaxy before refocusing on the road ahead of me.

I reached into my pocket and rolled the vial of black poison between my fingers. Over the last few days of traveling toward Scotland, I decided that my new mission was that of an ambassador. After all, if I killed humans, I might as well be working for Erebus.

I yawned, then blinked away the sleepy tears from my eyes. The border lay just ahead. Hopefully, I could find someplace decent to lodge for the night. I heard the Scottish barbarians slept in the dirt with pigs, that they fought naked in battle, and that they ate human flesh. I bit my lip. My heart raced faster as all the "what ifs" and rumors flooded my mind. I had to stop worrying before I convinced myself to turn back.

I pulled the hood of my cloak tighter around my face and watched the border draw near. The Scottish landscape didn't look any different than the scenery in England.

Although I didn't agree with assassination, I could see why Edward wanted to combine all the Britannia isles under one rule. If the Scots and Irish joined with the English, all the countries would be much stronger. It would be easier to protect the isles from invading armies, including the Shadow Legion.

My horse crossed the border. A frigid gust of wind hit me and tossed the hood of my cloak back. The mare shifted her weight and jumped from the sudden gale.

I pulled on the reins. "Whoa, girl." I patted the mare to reassure her. "It's just the wind." I pulled the hood over my head and continued north. The road thinned with claustrophobic malice. I stayed vigilant. The narrow road was the perfect place for an ambush.

Rowan branches reached out like claws and snagged my cloak and skirt. I fought against the tree and snapped a few branches. My horse snorted in irritation. I raised my hand and made my fist into a flaming torch to see the path ahead. I didn't usually use my powers for situations like this, but I was tired and just wanted to get out of the thicket. My paranoia was already getting the best of me as I imagined barbarians and wolves stalking me from the engulfing darkness. I urged the horse forward into a gallop. We broke through the worst of the bracken and charged into a clearing.

A bright flicker of light drew my gaze upward. Lamps blanketed a city on a hillside. "Gretna," I whispered. I would be safe staying here tonight. The English controlled Gretna and often used this town as a meeting place to collect taxes from the Scots.

I rode into the city, stopped at the first inn on the main road, and found an empty stall for my horse in the stable.

The horse nibbled on grain while I removed the saddle and hung it next to several other traditional English saddles. I smiled to myself. What a relief. Some of my fellow countrymen were here. If the Scots were as barbaric as everyone said they were, at least I would have reinforcements.

I entered the inn and pulled back the hood of my cloak. A fire danced in a pit and provided the only source of light in the dim room. A few men sat at the corner tables and leaned over mugs of foamy drinks. The stench of body odor, mildew, pipe smoke, and freshly baked bread hit my nose in an odiferous cocktail that made my stomach turn.

I strode toward the main counter where the innkeeper wiped a mug clean and set it on a shelf. I reached for my purse and pulled out a coin. "I need one bed for the night."

The bristly bearded innkeeper leaned forward and asked, "Are you travelin' alone, lass?" His Scottish accent came out thick, reminding me that I was mingling with the enemy.

I pulled three more shiny coins from my purse. The metal chimed against the counter. "These are for my three brothers. They will arrive any moment." I wasn't a good liar, but I hoped the other people in the room had heard my announcement and taken it seriously.

The room was silent as the men sipped their drinks and nibbled on the ends of their smoking pipes. One man's gaze darted away from mine when we made eye contact.

The innkeeper examined the coins as I held my breath, hoping he would accept the foreign money. It felt like everyone in the room watched me. The innkeeper took the coins, and then pointed up the stairs. "Third room on the right."

"Thank you," I whispered and headed toward the staircase.

Three men struggled at the top of the stairs. Two of them wore official English tunics that marked them as soldiers from my country. They snatched a young Scotsman and hurled him down the creaking staircase.

I dodged out of the way as the young man scrambled to his feet and raced for the exit.

The two English soldiers bounded down the stairs after him. A few men jumped up from the tables to help. I stood out of the way, completely confused by what was happening and why the soldiers were after the Scotsman.

The whole inn vibrated as the door slammed open. Several mugs fell from the shelves. The cups shattered and sparkling glass sprayed across the floor. Cold night air whirled around the room, removing what little heat the fire had made.

Lightning flashed and backlit a massive soldier. He stood like an ominous figure blocking the exit. The other men in the room stepped back, but still held weapons ready.

The soldiers surrounded the young Scotsman, slammed him against a table and held him down.

The massive soldier pulled out a sword and raised it above the young man's neck to kill him executioner style.

The Scottish men in the tavern came forward to save their own. It wasn't hard to see this would quickly turn into a blood bath.

"Stop!" I pushed them back and pulled the Scotsman off the table. No matter his crime, he deserved to be tried before the court and not beheaded on a tavern table. I turned to the soldiers and shouted, "What are you doing?" I couldn't believe the poor behavior of my own countrymen. I put my hands on my hips and waited for an answer. If King Edward truly wanted to unite our countries and avoid war, this was not the way to do it. This was an act of pure terror for all the witnesses—and the person who would have to clean up after the execution. "What was the crime worthy of beheading?" I asked.

One of the soldiers laughed and sized me up and down. "This Scottish scum tripped me."

"He tripped you?" I raised an eyebrow in disbelief and disgust. "So you're going to kill him?"

"He was defiant," another soldier justified.

"King Edward sent me here. We are to make peace with the Scottish and unite our countries, not terrorize them." I motioned toward the door and stood between the soldiers and the Scotsman, allowing him to escape.

"Why would King Edward send you?" The massive soldier scowled at me and his nostrils flared.

I wasn't going to let them intimidate me. "I am England's Watcher and outrank you thugs by several degrees. I intend to speak with your captain in the morning regarding your outrageous behavior."

"Watcher?" He growled. "That means you're Neviahan." His eyes flashed with fury. He yanked me toward him, whirled me around, and locked his arm across my throat. With my back against his chest, I tried to pry his forearm off me. His arm was as powerful as a python squeezing my neck as he flexed. My nails dug into his thick skin. His hot breath puffed over me. He sniffed my hair as if taking in my scent. The solider snarled as his lips flailed upward.

My fingers burned red hot with desperation. His flesh sizzled under my flaming Neviahan touch before he released me.

The massive solider licked the burns on his skin where I had branded his forearm in the shape of my hands. He lunged toward me again, sniffing the air, and then bared his teeth in a wide grin.

My heart pounded inside my chest. I reached for my sword.

"My lady," the innkeeper called loud enough for them to hear. "Your brothers are just up the stairs waiting for you. You better hurry or they'll worry for you, lass."

With weapons raised, several of the Scots were ready to come to my aid.

The soldiers must have realized they were outnumbered. They let down their aggressive stance and parted for me as if calling a temporary truce. I turned back and nodded my thanks to the innkeeper.

It seemed that the real barbarians in Scotland were my own countrymen. Edward would hear about this.

The fragile staircase creaked under my feet as I ascended. The shrill moan of decaying wood made me painfully self-conscious of my every move.

I walked down the hallway and found my assigned room. The ceiling was so low the only place I could stand erect was in the center where the roof pitched. There was no lock on the door to keep out intruders. I pressed my fingers against my temples in distress. This wasn't good. I had to somehow barricade the door if I wanted any security. I slid the bed across the room and hoped the adjustment in weight on the decrepit floor wouldn't make the bed fall through the brittle wood.

Once the bed was in place, I slowly sat down, listening to the cracks and creeks of a potential cave in. The hard mattress was about as comfortable as sleeping on the floor. No amount of yearning or sulking was going to make this situation better, and any thoughts of my plush bed in London would only depress me.

I kicked off my boots and unstrapped the scabbard and sword from my hips before lying down. I forced a smile on my face. "See, isn't this much better than sleeping in the dirt with pigs?"

This diplomatic mission was going to be harder than I thought. I had to be prepared for anything and couldn't trust anyone. Hopefully, the prejudice between the Scottish and the English wouldn't hinder me from meeting with the Scottish king. Besides, I was a lady and he was sure to be a gentleman and treat me honorably.

A tap came on my door. My heart skipped a beat, and I shot out of bed. The rapping grew louder and more insistent until the door shook under the beating. I pulled my sword close. Something was wrong. I slid the bed about an inch away from the door and held the sword ready at my side. I cracked open the door and peered out.

The young Scotsman I'd saved stood outside and looked up and down the hall. His hands balled into fists so tight the tendons in his forearms strained.

"May I help you?" I asked cautiously.

"You must get out o' here." His voice shook. "They're comin'."

I narrowed my eyes and gripped the edge of the door. "Who's coming?"

"The soldiers. I saw them in the woods. They're not men. They be Moddey Dhoo."

"Moddey Dhoo?" I asked. "What is Moddey Dhoo?"

The young man leaned forward and whispered, "Shadow Wolf."

As soon as I heard the name, my head whirled with dizziness. Fear gripped my stomach and my mouth went painfully dry. Shadow Lords I could handle with ease, but the Shadow Wolves paralyzed me with terror. Memories I had tried to forget flooded my mind. I was only thirteen and knew nothing of Neviah or the Shadow Legion when I was first attacked. My leg had been mangled by Erebus's alpha wolf. It was a year before I could walk properly again. I reached up and touched the faint scar across my temple. I would never forget the mind breaking horror when they had started to eat me alive.

"There's a whole pack of Shadow Wolves coming for you, lass. You must leave now," the Scotsman urged.

I strapped on my belt. I wouldn't have much of a head start. The wolves could be outside waiting for me now. I hopped on one foot, trying to pull my boot on. The scabbard flapped against my side, tripping me, and I tumbled onto the bed.

I shoved my other foot into the second boot. My fingers quivered as I laced the ties unevenly and wound the strings into several knots.

I hurled the bed away from the door and raced down the hallway. My boots pressed awkwardly on my little toes. I looked down and rolled my eyes. My boots were on the wrong feet. There was no time to correct that mistake now.

"The innkeeper is getting your horse ready."

I raced for the door. The Scotsman grabbed my hand and pulled me toward the back of the inn. "Don't go that way," he informed and motioned toward the kitchen.

I followed him through the kitchen, and we burst through the back door. The innkeeper waited with my horse, bridled and saddled.

The cold wind whipped around me. Dark mists swirled across the muddy road. The wolves were close. The air grew colder and the sky darker.

The young Scotsman boosted me into the saddle.

"Thank you," I said. I don't know what I would have done if he hadn't warned me.

"No, thank you for standing up to those soldiers," he said. "I've never been saved by a woman before."

The innkeeper chuckled. "I guess not all you English types are rotten."

I shook my head. "No, we aren't. Thank you. I will never forget your kindness."

A howl echoed, shattering our farewell.

I kicked the sides of my midnight black horse and took off at a gallop. Storm clouds blanketed the stars, darkening the world in an obsidian sheet. I reached the outer rim of the city, and the road curved northeast toward Edinburgh.

Howling and yelps broke the eerie silence of the night and resonated in quick, low wails. They had my scent. Panic sprang from the pit of my stomach and stole the moisture from my mouth. My wet hands gripped the reins tighter.

"Yah!" I called and urged the horse into a full sprint. Clods of mud flung into the air behind my mare's hooves as she galloped down the slick road.

Another wolf howled from the south. I glanced over my shoulder. Six wolves, as tall as my horse, bounded behind me. Their red eyes blazed with hunger like hell's lanterns.

I clenched my teeth and held out my hand. A stream of fire shot from my fingertips in their direction. The flames lit up the woods, revealing spiny trees and more wolves racing with the main pack. The beasts dodged my fiery assault.

"Nine wolves," I whispered to myself. The most I had ever fought at once was three, and that had been a close competition.

I could hear them now, panting behind me and snapping at the mare's legs. The scent of carnage hit my nose.

"Yah!" I desperately urged my horse to run faster, but she was already exhausted from the day's trip. I couldn't outrun the wolves. My only choice was to lose them in the woods. I veered toward the unfamiliar forest. Wet brush slapped past my legs. The wolves stayed on my blazed trail, dodging between trees and racing alongside me.

I drew my sword and looked from the wolf on my right to the one on the left, desperately trying to ascertain a battle plan. The forest gave way to a clearing. Two wolves simultaneously lunged for me as if they had planned and practiced how to execute the assault.

I extended my sword while shooting a ball of fire in the other direction. The pressure of crunching bone and tearing flesh vibrated up my arm as the lunging wolf skewered itself on my blade. I lowered the weapon and let the weight of the dead body slip off my sword as my horse continued to gallop.

The second wolf whirled as if trying to shake the flames from its back. It charged like a flaming battering ram into my steed. My horse reared from the attack. I clung onto the saddle and gained control of the injured mare. I commanded her forward, her gallop uneven now.

A deep gorge marked the clearing like an unnatural scar on the Earth. I pulled back on the reins, stopping my horse before I plummeted into its depths. A river raged along the bottom like a death trap.

The alpha wolf emerged from the forest. Shadows billowed off his wild fur, as if he emanated black fog. Red light flashed in his eyes. His massive paws hit the mud, but left no prints. "It's over—you're trapped," he said. I recognized his hoarse voice. He was the soldier who had taken my scent at the inn.

I raised my sword defiantly. "I won't be held prisoner." I'd rather die than be captured and tortured again.

"Of course," the wolf's voice dropped to a low growl. "We weren't ordered to take you prisoner. You have been marked by Erebus for death."

The ground rumbled and lightning whipped across the sky. Rain dropped in frigid waves.

I glanced behind me at the deep gorge and raging river. If I could make it to the other side, I could lose them.

I shot another stream of fire at the wolves. My golden firelight reflected off a million raindrops like a torch igniting in a crystal cave. The flames whirled around the alpha male in a sphere of heat.

One of the smaller wolves lunged for me. The momentum of the attack threw me back and knocked me off the horse. My head slammed against the ground. I blinked once to shake off the assault, just as the wolf's gaping mouth of dagger-like teeth opened wide and plunged toward my face.

I gripped the beast's massive head with smoldering fingers and dug my nails into his eyes. The wolf jerked back. I rolled to press myself up into a stand. Another wolf's teeth sank deep into my arm.

It shook its head, ripping my flesh apart. I screamed and beat against the Shadow Wolf with my fist. It flung me onto the muddy ground. My shoulder snapped and searing pain raced across my chest and down my back. Every nerve in my body shrieked with torment.

I burst into flames, the wolf released its grip, and I scrambled to my feet. I had to get away while I still had the strength to summon my Neviahan power. I turned my feet sideways and slid down the muddy slope of the gorge to the river below. My hand trailed behind me, catching on twigs and rocks as I tried to balance myself in the rapid descent. The wolves wouldn't dare submerge themselves into the water. The rain was probably torture enough. The Rebellion avoided water as much as they avoided sunlight. Pure water was one of the Shadow Legion's weaknesses; unfortunately, it was my weakness as well.

I glanced over my shoulder. The wolves bounded down the hillside after me. The sound of the river below grew louder and drowned out the howling and snarling. It was my only chance of escape.

My feet sank into the river. The shock of icy waves stung my skin. My long skirt soaked up the frigid water like a wick. I hurled myself into the rapids and plunged below the waves. The torrent battered me as I desperately clawed against the current to reach a breath of air. My head emerged from the river and I gasped. The remaining wolves raced along the bank.

Bolts of lightning struck the earth. Wind whirled around me. The river rapids grew faster and whipped me through the maze of sharp rocks.

It seemed that even the river warred against me. The currents hurled me into a cluster of boulders. I clung to the jagged rocks protruding out of the water and flexed my toes, trying to keep the current from ripping the hastily tied boots off my feet.

The river rushed passed me in icy waves. I took in quick breaths when the water momentarily broke from slamming against my face.

Mists of darkness swirled around the wolves pacing on the bank. "How long do you think you can hold on?" a wolf taunted.

I coughed and sucked in more of the river. I had to pull myself out of the water and make it to the far bank. My injured shoulder and arm burned with agony. I could do this. I had to. I clawed at the rock until my fingers burned. Hot sparks from my fingernails showered off the stone each time I slid back. I tried to ignore the pain and focus on the bank. It was just over a meter away. I reached out with my leg, pointing my toes to try to balance myself onto the shore. I could almost reach it.

I prepared to fight my way through the river to the other side. I pulled back for more momentum and heard something snap. A large tree branch rolled toward me. Like a massive enemy hand, it ripped me from the rock and held me under the river.

Below the surface, I held my breath and struggled with the web of wood, breaking the limbs, trying to escape the grasp. My cold hands trembled, my lungs burned. I felt my engagement ring slip from my finger. I fumble in the water, trying to catch the ring Lucas had given me. I saw it glint as the current carried it away.

I couldn't do this anymore. My powers were null under the waves; I was injured, I had no strength left, and now I had lost my engagement ring. Panic took over.

The water rushed around me. I snapped a few branches out of frustration, but couldn't free myself. My lungs ached as I surrendered my last breath to the flood.

Chapter Five

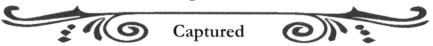

Captured

I could feel their teeth ripping into my flesh, sinking past the muscle and gnawing on my bone. I screamed and grabbed my leg. This was an all-too familiar dream. I was only thirteen when Hazella, a Watcher gone bad, captured me and tortured me for information about my powers. That time in my life was over, but the nightmares still continued.

My eyes sprang open. Air flowed into my lungs with ease, drowning out the fear I remembered before everything had gone black. My heart pounded as loud as the pain pulsing from my brow.

By the stone walls and faint light, it seemed that I was underground or in a cave. I was grateful for the dim light or my headache would have turned into a warzone behind my skull.

I didn't dare sit up or move too fast, but I touched the smooth quilt wrapped around my beaten body. Reaching farther, my fingertips brushed along the silky fur of a great beast. Images of Shadow Wolves flooded my mind. I shot up. My vision swirled with dizziness.

A massive white tiger raised its head and perked its ears forward. I hadn't expected this. I froze in place and stared into the pale blue eyes of the great cat. The tiger was so wide and thick I could have ridden it like a horse. The cat's head was the size of a shield. I had no doubt its teeth were as long as daggers. A faint spot of sunlight came from behind me at the cave entrance. Did I have a chance of escaping the tiger's den?

Ignoring my injuries, I slid toward the mouth of the cave with slow, controlled movements as my eyes adjusted to the light. My hand hit a candlestick. It clanked against the stone floor and rolled toward the giant cat. My heart sprinted, and I held my breath, waiting for the beast to pounce. The cat sniffed the candlestick, looked up, and blinked with sleepy eyes.

Bright red blood soaked the tiger's coat across its striped shoulders. It was hurt. I recognized the cruel pattern of the wound. "The wolves," I realized. The tiger must have saved me, but why? The great cat was the size of Erebus's largest alpha wolf and could have easily devoured me if it wanted. The tiger lowered its head submissively. I had seen house cats do the same thing when they wanted affection.

I lifted my hand and reached toward the great beast with cautious fingers. "Nice kitty," my voice quivered. My trembling hand sank into the white fur. The cat rolled onto its back. I jerked away at the sudden movement.

The tiger blinked at me and curled its massive paws, begging to have its belly rubbed. I relaxed, slid toward the tiger, and stroked the colossal kitty's fluffy stomach.

The tiger let out a playful rumble deep in its throat that almost sounded like a satisfied purr. How adorable. I wondered if King Edward would let me keep it as a pet in the castle. I leaned into the beast's warm body and noticed clean bandages lining my arm where the wolf had bitten me. Apparently the tiger wasn't the only one who had saved me.

My gaze darted around the cave. Bags of traveling gear, clothing, a pair of muddy boots, and several swords filled the void. "You're already someone's pet?" I asked the tiger. The tiger narrowed its eyes and looked offended. "Oh, sorry," I apologized for the unintended insult. "I suppose you are too majestic to be a pet."

The tiger perked its ears forward. Its whiskers lifted proudly.

"Thank you for saving me," I said and continued to stroke the tiger's fur.

A deep masculine voice shattered the silence of the cave. "Don't let him take all the credit for saving you."

I jumped and whirled around to face the stranger. Backlit by the cave entrance, a white aura swirled around the man's silhouette as if he were a god from mythological tales. I held my hand to my face, shielding my eyes as they adjusted to the light he radiated.

The man knelt beside me and reached for my hand. I pulled away, slid back against the wall, and focused on his features. A dark mask lined his handsome face over his familiar, shimmering eyes.

"Who are you?" I tried not to sound suspicious, but he seemed too beautiful to be human.

"My name 'tis Azrael." His calm voice soothed like royal velvet. "I am Scotland's Watcher."

"You are a Watcher?" I could hardly breathe. Finally, someone like me.

He nodded.

I didn't doubt he was telling the truth. He was not human, though he was in a human body, and the enemy couldn't radiate light the way he did. Here was someone who understood who I really was. We were the same. I suddenly felt liberated from the human world with a sense of belonging. My veins rush with unearthly energy like I was being cured of homesickness. "I've never met another Watcher before." I searched his features, looking for part of myself in him— the non-human part.

"Like you?" He smiled and shook his head to disagree. "I may be a Watcher, but I'm not as fair or delicate as you are, m'lady."

Looking down at my damaged arm, I couldn't deny his statement about being delicate, but I didn't believe I was as fair as the god-like warrior.

I cringed, thinking how I must appear to him. My arm looked awful, and I could only imagine the ruins the rest of my body was in.

Azrael reached for my hand. A blue spark shot from his fingertips to mine. I jerked away, but he grasped my hand and kissed the top in a perfect, gentlemanly way. He lifted his eyes, but kept his lips close to my hand. I could feel his breath as he spoke. "I am overjoyed at finding you."

I recoiled my hand. "How did you find me?" I asked, shying away from his admiring gaze.

His eyes danced with amusement behind his mask. "I simply thought of the most trouble you could get into and knew you would find a way to make it happen."

I smiled sheepishly. He had me there. "Where are the Shadow Wolves?" I asked, hoping to learn of what happened after everything went black under the raging river. Every horrible scenario started playing through my imagination.

"The Blood Hunters are dead. Orion, Korban, and I slew the rest."

"Blood Hunters?" I asked.

"Blood Hunters, Shadow Wolves, Hell Hounds, Moddey Dhoo, they're all the same thing," Azrael said.

"Just three of you took on all those Blood Hunters?" I said, using the same perfect term to describe the beasts.

The tiger lifted his head and turned one ear back while perking his whiskers forward.

Azrael scratched the tiger between the ears, then added, "And the cat, too."

The tiger seemed pleased with the acknowledgement and laid his head back down on his paw.

"It wasn't that difficult," Azrael said. "You killed four of the wolves before we got to you."

"Four?" I whispered, and smiled. That was a new record for me.

Azrael nodded. "Even the alpha wolf was completely scorched when we got to the site. You have a remarkable power inside you."

I beamed, still amazed that I had killed four wolves in the chaos, including the alpha wolf. I sat a little taller and felt more like a warrior.

Azrael took my hand. His celestial energy absorbed into my skin like the intense warmth of a campfire on a cold night. "After you eat, I need to drain the venom pooling in your arm." He ran his fingers along my bandage.

"Venom?" I gasped. That explained the searing burning in my forearm.

Azrael nodded. "Yes, from one of Erebus's wolves." Past the mask hiding his face, he stared into my eyes as if looking into my soul. I felt completely exposed under his intense gaze. "Your fire gift is not only a weapon, but it can also heal your wounds." Azrael explained, "After the tiger pulled you to shore, I examined the extent of your injuries. You already healed your arm with fire during the battle, 'tis how I knew of your healing gift." He nodded to my shoulder. "I assumed you could only heal flesh wounds since your shoulder is still dislocated. I suppose your ability to mend your open wounds is a way to protect your precious blood from the Shadow Lords who crave it."

"You're brilliant," I praised his accurate evaluation. Usually I wore my ruby necklace to heal bruises, sprains, breaks, and other injuries that didn't involve torn flesh.

Azrael's lips twitched into a smile before he turned serious again. "The real problem is the venom from the Blood Hunter's bite. I put some salve on it to slow the effects, but I need to cut your arm open again to drain it out."

I took a deep breath and imagined the painful procedure that loomed in my near future.

"You are only mortal, but for a mortal you are still more powerful than even the Immortals."

I smiled at the exaggerated compliment. I had heard stories about the Immortals. I was nothing like them.

Voices came from outside the cave and two silhouettes stepped in front of the entrance, blocking the light.

"What're we goin' to do with the assassin?" a man with a thick Scottish accent asked in a cheerful tone.

The second man laughed. "She's a lot prettier than I thought she'd be. If England's assassins are all like her, I hope a few will come after me."

I put my hand to my forehead. What a disaster! How many people knew about my ridiculous assassination mission?

Azrael's mouth turned up in one corner. "Meet Orion and Korban."

I remembered Azrael mentioning them. The two men were just as god-like and beautiful as Azrael. I noticed all three wore traditional Scottish kilts and plaid sashes. Leather straps crossed over their varying earth-toned, short sleeve shirts to hold their weapons on their backs.

My heart sank as I thought of the misguided, Scottish monarchy they were forced to protect. From what I heard, their barbarian king was more war-hungry than Edward.

Azrael motioned toward the short, slender man with messy, black hair and chiseled features. "Korban is the best swordsman in the twelve Neviahan galaxies. His gift is to wield any kind of weapon."

Korban flashed me a smile. His deep brown eyes sparkled with pride.

Azrael pointed to the tall, broad-shouldered man who filled most of the cave when he stepped inside. "And this is Orion."

Evaluating his size, I expected his gift to be something to do with strength, especially since he carried a massive battle axe with a blade as large as a shield.

Korban elbowed Orion in the ribs. "Aye, he can make flowers grow. 'Tis his powers."

Orion narrowed his eyes and crossed his thick, muscular arms. "You weren't complainin' when thistles attacked the Norse and saved all yer scrawny hides."

Azrael expounded, "Orion is a Watcher with earth elemental powers."

Orion turned to me. "We hear you 'ave the fire element."

I nodded and searched their expressions for any sign of fear. I was used to the way humans reacted to me and my abilities, but there was only delight in their eyes. "Who is the tiger?" I asked.

Azrael rubbed the tiger in between his ears. "This is Baby. He is my animal companion. Most Watchers eventually get an animal companion or a special trinket of sorts to help them with their quests."

"Baby?" That wasn't the name I expected for a tiger that looked like he could swallow a man whole. I patted the heroic cat. "Thank you for pulling me from the river, Baby." The tiger's grin grew wide. I turned to the men and formally introduced myself, "I am Lady Auriella."

"We know," Orion said and shrugged his shoulders like he didn't care. "But we've been calling you Aura this whole time, so don't expect us to stop now."

"Aura?" I was surprised by their casualness in addressing me and the fact that they already knew my name.

Azrael grinned, "'Tis easier than Lady Auriella."

I could go with the name. It was then I realized I had seen the name 'Aura' on the letter warning me of Erebus's attack. They knew this would happen. "You were the ones who warned me about the Blood Hunters," I said.

"We've been after that pack of dogs for months now," Orion said. "'Twas our pleasure, lass."

Korban let out a chuckle. "More Azrael's pleasure. He was the one who resuscitated you after you nearly drowned in the river."

My eyes flew open wide with horror. Korban had to be joking.

Azrael's expression radiated something mischievous. "Forgive me. I was hoping our first kiss would be a bit more romantic."

First kiss? I tightened my jaw and tried not to envision his mouth over mine. I shook my head, but my heart took off at a sprint. Hot Neviahan blood rushed through my veins. I couldn't stop staring at his terrifying, yet perfect mouth.

I forced myself to sound regal, hard, and indifferent. "It wasn't a kiss if I didn't give it willingly." It's not like I could ever have a relationship with him. I belonged to England and to Lucas. Besides Azrael worked for the barbarian enemy. Although right now, I was the one who looked more like a barbarian. My filthy hands were caked in blood. My hair was probably just as ravaged as my clothing. Embarrassment washed over me. I couldn't believe anyone had seen me this way, and I was horrified that Azrael had "kissed" me while I was in this condition. "I need a moment to collect myself," I said in a small voice.

"That means she wants us to leave, huh?" Orion asked Korban.

I nodded. Azrael ushered the other men out, but seemed hesitant to leave himself. "Are you upset about . . .?" Azrael pointed to his lips.

I shook my head quickly, but didn't say anything. I didn't know what to say.

Azrael didn't look convinced by my answer. He turned and the air grew colder as he walked farther away.

Dropping my shoulders, I released the breath I didn't know I held. I made sure the men were out of sight before kneeling beside the bucket of icy water. My pathetic reflection floated across the surface. I saw why my head pounded. A bump crowned my brow where I had hit the rocks. My hair hung in tangles around my bruised face. I looked like I had been thrown off a cliff.

Cringing, I put my finger into the bucket, shattering my pitiful reflection. I tried to summon the heat of my elemental power to warm the water. I closed my eyes and concentrated, but no fire came from my hands. My power and energy seemed to always run out after a long, hard fight. My shoulders dropped in defeat. I cupped the shimmering water in my hands and splashed my face with the shockingly cold liquid.

I tried to relax and fight the pain and embarrassment from the attack. My arm burned, making me keenly aware of the venom pulsing inside my flesh. Baby nudged me and slipped his head under my arm to comfort me. I was sure the intuitive tiger sensed my discouragement. With my good hand, I stroked his fur and rubbed his ears. "You're just a friendly, big kitty, aren't you?"

I took a rag and washed the wounds on Baby's shoulder.

Baby moaned dramatically. I could tell the cat loved the attention I gave him, so I fed his ego by oohing and awing over his bravery. Baby suddenly perked up and licked his chops. I could smell it too. We followed the scent of roasting meat to the cave entrance.

Azrael, Orion, and Korban talked next to a fire. A small roast cooked above the flames. My horse grazed in the forest next to three others. I let out a sigh of relief. I thought for sure the Blood Hunters had eaten her. I could tell by the number of bandages covering my horse, it would be a while before I could ride her again.

Azrael glanced toward the cave and saw me watching them. He deftly jumped to his feet and bounded toward me with a wide grin. "You look beautiful." His gaze struck me with wonder as if he wanted to tell me something, but couldn't. "Come by the fire, and get something warm to eat," he offered.

When he touched my hand, something ancient burned inside me as if hidden power was being resurrected. I pulled away from Azrael's comforting grasp and stepped from the cave entrance. I didn't know how to repress these haunting feelings I didn't understand.

"Where are your shoes?" he asked.

I let out a quick laugh. "I must have lost them in the river."

Azrael made a quick turn and my feet swung off the ground. I gasped and clutched onto his shoulder as he carried me in his arms as if I were weightless. "There, you don't need shoes now," Azrael stated.

I covered my face with one hand. "I can't believe you are doing this."

"Doing what?" he asked with false innocence.

"Carrying me," I said and didn't hide the irritation. "I'm not a damsel in distress, I'm a knight."

His eyes danced with laughter. "'Tis called chivalry. I'm sure you were taught chivalry in knight school. Did they not teach you to accept chivalry as well?" His Scottish accent came out thick.

Knight school? I couldn't tell if he was mocking traditional English knighthood or not. Who knew what the Scottish enemies had told him about the English.

Azrael set me on a deerskin beside the fire and sat across from me. He picked up a straight stick and fastened an arrowhead to the end. I tried to examine more of his features behind his black mask and a week's worth of stubble covering his firm jaw-line.

Orion turned the roast over the fire and Korban ran a sharpening stone over the edge of his sword. Energy flew from the woods toward the three men as if they were magnets for light. I had never seen such strong energy forces. Were all Watcher men like this? I must look so plain and ordinary to them.

The sun broke through the clouds and splashed across my opal skin, making me glitter like a fairy. Azrael's gaze shot up and Orion shifted his weight. Even Korban stopped sharpening his sword. They held perfectly still, not even breathing as they all stared at me.

My ivory skin shimmered with specks of rose, gold, emerald, and lavender in the sunlight. Brushing my arm, I looked away. I seldom thought about my strange opal-like skin because I was the only one who ever saw the phenomenon. Humans and the Shadow Legion couldn't see the Neviahan mark, but Azrael, Orion, and Korban obviously noticed.

I glanced at the three men. None of them sparkled like I did. Why was my skin so different from theirs? This couldn't be good. I realized that even among my own kind, I was an oddity. I had to get out of the sunlight. I swallowed hard and tried to sound casual. "Excuse me." I jumped to my feet and marched toward the cave. A wave of dizziness hit me like a tsunami. I swayed, trying to catch my balance as the world spun around me.

Azrael grasped my arm and forced me to sit. "Quick, she needs something to eat."

Korban took his knife and carved off a generous portion of the roast.

"I think I am just tired," I said. I winced against the nauseating pain of my dislocated shoulder and the venom burning in my arm.

Azrael stared at the bandages around my arm. "You've lost a lot of blood, and the venom is attacking your body."

Orion nodded in agreement. "She's pale as the moon. This'll hinder our mission. Do you think she'll make it to the sanctuary?"

"Your mission? Sanctuary?" I didn't hide my anxiety at the hint of their agenda. "I have my own mission to accomplish."

"We need to drain the venom," Azrael said, ignoring my worry. "It'll be a few days before we can travel again."

"Wait. Where are we going?" I asked with more force.

Korban passed the bowl to Azrael, and he handed it to me. My hand grazed across Azrael's. A blue spark flew from his outstretched fingers to mine and lit our faces. I could tell by their stunned expressions that Korban and Orion had seen and heard the flash of energy too.

Azrael leaned away, his face flushed, and he brushed his hair back with one hand. "It must be energy left over from the storm last night." His voice quaked, though he grinned wide with amusement.

"Must be." I did not hide the suspicion in my voice. There was something strange about the three Watchers, and I was going to discover their secret and agenda.

They were too charming to be common thieves, too rugged to be noble knights, and their masculine frames, sculpted for battle, left out the possibility of them being lazy lords. They claimed to be Neviahan, but why were these Watchers so different from me?

Chapter Six

 Venom

I had eaten more than a lady's share of venison, and Baby devoured the rest of the meal. Azrael, Orion, and Korban refused to eat anything, which made me only more nervous as they watched me eat. Azrael couldn't keep his eyes off my shimmering skin. Orion and Korban pretended not to be bothered by me, but they jerked uneasily every time I shifted in the sunlight. Something about my Neviahan mark upset them. The dizziness left me, but excitement, confusion, intrigue, and fear meshed together in my heart as I retreated out of the sun and back into the cave.

Right now, I had a bigger problem to worry about. I bit on my lower lip, trying to suppress the throbbing pain from my dislocated shoulder and the burning venom in my arm. My fingers strained, trying to create an amber flame. Hopefully, the heat would dull the pain. A spark sputtered from my fingertips, then went out. I was still too weak to summon that kind of energy. I balled my hands into fists and leaned against the cave wall. For a split second, I wished I had my healing ruby necklace, but I didn't regret my decision to give it to

Lucas. I imagined him, a human, fighting against the assailing Shadow Legion. I shouldn't have left him alone. Perhaps I could convince Azrael, Orion, and Korban to come and aid us in London.

"How are you feeling, now that you've had a good meal?" Azrael asked.

Startled by his entrance into the cave, I whirled around. Azrael knelt beside me and slid close. Baby plopped down and laid his massive head in my lap.

"I'm fine," I said cheerfully and forced a smile on my face.

Azrael reached for my hand. I pulled away, not wanting him to touch my skin in or out of the sunlight. I had never been so self-conscious about the way my skin looked.

"I want to see your arm." Azrael gripped my wrist with a gentle firmness from which I didn't dare pull away. I watched his expression as he unraveled the bandages to reveal where the Shadow Wolf had bitten me. The smell of rotting flesh could not be hidden. Red and purple lines ran like trails up my arm.

Azrael pulled away. He wasn't smiling. His knuckles whitened, and he swallowed hard. "'Tis not good. Wolf venom is meant to slow you down so they can hunt you easier. The scent is potent to the Legion. They can track a Neviahan injected with venom for miles." He swallowed hard and continued, "'Tis a cruel death that lasts over a matter of days." Azrael smiled gently, though his eyes saddened. "But you are not going to die. We are going to draw out the venom."

My tongue curled at the gruesome thought of reopening my arm. I pinched my eyebrows together and forced my voice to stay steady. "Is there another way?"

Azrael shook his head. "No, and if I'm not able to get all the venom out, our only other option is to . . ." He glanced at a sword propped in the corner.

"Don't say it." I repressed the ghastly image of having my arm amputated.

"I will do everything in my power to help you," Azrael assured. "Stay here." He jumped to his feet and darted from the cave.

I took several deep breaths and turned to Baby. "Does Azrael have physician training?"

The cat rolled his eyes.

I laughed—something I always did when nervous. I didn't want just anyone cutting into my arm.

Baby dropped his head in my lap. I ran my fingers through his fur. "If what Azrael said is true about Watchers getting animal companions, I hope my animal will be as cute as you, Baby."

Baby licked my hand with his rough tongue.

Azrael returned with a heavy wooden bucket. Black ash covered the bottom and steam rose from the water. He dropped a dagger into the boiling water to sanitize the blade. "Before we drain the venom, I'm going to snap your shoulder back into place."

"Snap?" I repeated uneasily.

Azrael shook his head. "That wasn't a good word to use. I'm going to set your shoulder where it should be."

It was too late; he had already said "snap". I braced myself and touched his hand, expecting to be shocked again. This time I only felt his warm fingers slip between mine.

"Are you ready?" he asked.

I nodded.

Azrael slid his other hand under my arm and braced my shoulder. He pulled our interlocked hands toward him while pushing my shoulder up.

The pain grew more intense. My teeth ground together. I held my breath to keep from gasping. A loud "snap" came from my shoulder. "Arg!" I let out a scream and dropped my head. I took several deep breaths while the pain dulled. "That's better," I sighed.

"That was the easy part," Azrael murmured. "After we get the venom out, I will make a sling for your arm."

I leaned back against the wall and rubbed my shoulder, hoping to massage the pain away.

"Does it still hurt?" he asked.

"It's a little tender, but it feels much better."

"I have an idea of something that might help." Azrael leaned forward. His eyes sparkled behind his dark mask. "Now don't be frightened," he warned.

I couldn't stand the mask covering his eyes. What was he hiding anyway? I swallowed hard before asking, "Why would I be frightened?"

A small, golden flame burst from his hand. I jumped and slammed my back against the cave wall. Did I just see what I thought I saw? The fire flickered in his hands like gold energy. I gazed at the warm light beaming across his face. I held my breath and examined Azrael as if I was seeing him for the first time.

"Shhh." Azrael closed his hand around the flame and smothered it. "Don't be frightened."

"You're a fire Watcher like me." My words came out in a gasp. No wonder I felt such a deep connection with him.

Azrael nodded. "'Tis only a minor gift. My fire powers are not nearly as powerful as yours."

"Minor gift?" I asked. "You have more than one?"

Azrael nodded. "Of course. Our gifts are like talents. Though most of us are born with a natural power, we can develop many gifts. We are not limited."

Azrael held out his hand once more. A flame ignited from his palm. My lips turned up in a wide grin. Warm shadows danced on the cave walls as the fire flickered in his hands. He watched me as if gauging my reaction. "Please," Azrael begged. "Don't be frightened."

I shook my head. "I'm not frightened." This time I really meant it.

Azrael pressed the flame onto my shoulder. His heat penetrated deep into my flesh, flowing through my body like hot steam. The pain subsided as tranquility washed over me in waves. I closed my eyes and enjoyed the moment.

"Better?" Azrael asked, pulling away.

My head bobbed as I nodded. I'd never felt so relaxed. It took effort to sit up straight so I wouldn't fall asleep. "It feels . . . amazing."

"Good. That was the easy injury to heal." Azrael touched the handle of the dagger and pulled it from the boiling water. He let out a long sigh and took my hand. "I will have to make six incisions: three on the top of your arm and three on the bottom. Then I will use hot rags to draw the venom out."

I braced myself. "I'm ready." I tried to keep my voice sure and courageous.

Azrael held the tip of the blade to my arm. I squinted my eyes at the sharp prick. Azrael sucked in a quick breath, bracing himself as well. Hot metal pressed into my delicate skin and broke through the layers of flesh. My blood sizzled against the hot knife and black liquid bubbled from my forearm. I clenched my teeth together and pressed my lips tight to keep from screaming. Adrenaline rushed through my veins. My toes curled in agony. My nerves burned and my ears pounded, matching the erratic sound of my thumping heart.

"There," Azrael finally said.

I exhaled and opened my eyes. Black tar-like goo covered his hand and dripped off the edge of the blade.

"Is that the venom?" I asked, horrified by the shadowy color.

Azrael nodded and dropped the dagger into the water. "'Tis all going to come out. I promise." He held a sweltering rag to the first incision on my arm.

My breath caught and I leaned my head against the cave wall. "Azrael, did you make all six cuts?" I kept my voice indifferent. I didn't want to sound like I was complaining, but I didn't want to do that again.

"I only made three cuts on the top of your arm. Once I clean them, I will start on the other three."

I swallowed. Sweat glistened on my face and hot tears threatened to spill out my eyes. It was only half over. I looked away, gripped Azrael's hand, and clenched my teeth. Steam rose from my arm as the heat cleansed the wounds. It was a painful heat, nothing like Azrael's elemental touch.

"You are so courageous," Azrael encouraged.

My eyes watered. I took in a short breath and pretended it didn't hurt as much as it did. I struggled to keep from jerking my arm away from him.

Azrael finally pulled the cloth from the lesion. I expected to see blood, but instead more black venom soaked the cloth.

I pulled a disgusted face.

"There's more venom than I thought." Azrael took another hot rag from the bucket and put it into my arm.

The intense agony seemed to burn every nerve in my body. I had to do something to distract myself from the torture. I tried to start a conversation and blurted the first thing that came to my mind. "Why doesn't your skin shimmer in the sunlight like mine does?"

Azrael's lips twitched as he repressed a smile. I hoped I hadn't offended him by the question. "I'm a man," he answered. Heat penetrated deep into my flesh, cleansing muscle and tissue. Azrael continued, "Only the women of our kind carry the Lifelight."

"Lifelight?" I asked through clenched teeth. Azrael pulled the rag from my arm. Red blood finally tinted the cloth in a small patch.

"The Lifelight means you can have children."

"Oh," I replied and swallowed an awkward lump in my throat.

"The Shadow Legion can't see it and neither can humans, not unless they get really close to you in the sunlight." He paused and concentrated on planting another scorching rag into my arm. I held my breath.

Azrael continued, "Neviahan men are the ones who can see the Lifelight most prominently." His lips turned up in one corner before his smile broadened. "'Tis an attractive lure for a potential mate."

Sudden heat rose to my face, from more than just the treatment. That would explain the men's reaction to me earlier. Steam billowed out of my arm and dewed like hot rain on the cave walls. Azrael didn't seem embarrassed as he concentrated on cleaning the wound.

I studied his face. Aside from being almost god-like in strength and masculine beauty, he looked like any other normal human. If I looked as human as Azrael did, no wonder people kept forgetting I was not from Earth, but from the Kingdom of Neviah. Our human bodies were the perfect disguise for our souls. I smiled to myself, forgetting about the pain. I would never be alone again. Not only did I find others like me, but another Neviahan Watcher with the same power I had. "I've been waiting a long time to meet someone like you."

Azrael let out a low chuckle. "Not nearly as long as I've been waiting to see you."

His sincere, genuine tone made me smile. Azrael removed the hot rag from my wound. "We need to heat the water again before we do the other side." He gave me a canteen of water to drink from and took the bucket outside.

I sipped on the cold liquid until Azrael returned with the reheated water.

"Can you use your fire and burn out the venom?" I asked. I didn't want to have to go through that pain all over again.

Azrael shook his head. "'Tis too dangerous."

"You're not going to hurt me." I was sure of that. I craved to feel his fire again.

"'Tis not that." Azrael gave me an attractive half smile. "I'm worried you might hurt me."

I was confused. Why would I hurt him?

Azrael continued, "And you might kill every living thing within a hundred leagues of this place. My fire can never touch your blood."

I held my wounded arm close to my body, horrified by the destruction of which he claimed I was capable.

Azrael pulled the dagger from the boiling water and reached for my arm. "'Tis alright," he said. "I'm not going to light your blood on fire."

I was still hesitant, but held out my arm to him.

"How much do you know about the prophecy of the Lady of Neviah?" he asked.

I gritted my teeth and tried to murmur past the pain of the knife slicing through my flesh. "I am she." Or at least that's what I had been told by Woldor, the Neviahan Historian. The pain seemed to suffocate me until my lungs burned for air. My fingernails scraped against the cave floor. I tightened the muscles in my legs to keep from writhing.

Azrael set the knife down and took a hot rag from the bucket. "You are the Great Kingdom of Neviah's secret weapon."

I exhaled and tried to make light of his exaggerated admiration. "I make a lousy secret weapon."

Azrael chuckled and pulled the cloth covered in black stains from my arm. "No, you just haven't unlocked your full powers yet."

"What do you mean?" I asked before he shoved another scorching rag into my arm. I winced and bit down on my lip.

"My natural power is not to control fire," he explained. "I had to learn from the high druids how to use fire so I could help you in battle."

"You are going to help me in battle?" I was sure Azrael didn't understand a word I said through my clenched teeth.

"You have the power of Starfire. 'Tis all the elements of creation combined—fire, water, wind, earth, blood, life, and death. If Erebus stole Starfire, he could conquer Earth in a matter of days."

I clenched my fists. Azrael pulled the black-spotted cloth from my arm. I wiped the perspiration from my face with my fingertips

"Starfire has extra protection. Now hold still, we're almost done." I gritted my teeth and Azrael dug the rag into my arm to scrape out the last of the venom. "Not only can your fire mend your flesh to protect your blood from Erebus, but you only carry one half of the Starfire power," he explained. "There is another Neviahan with the power of Starfire. Unless Erebus combines both their blood, he can't use Starfire—no one can."

I gripped my leg to keep myself from ripping my wounded arm away from Azrael. "Is that why I've only created ordinary fire so far?"

Azrael nodded. "You need to combine your power with your 'key' to create Starfire – the secret weapon."

"Key?" I asked and squeezed my eyes shut, trying to block out the pain.

"Yes. You are the fuel, and the key is the igniter to start the inferno inside you." Azrael pulled the rag from my arm. "There."

I opened my eyes and noted the blood-stained cloth.

Azrael smiled and looked satisfied. "We got all the venom out."

I laid my head against the wall, letting out a long sigh.

"Do you have enough energy to close up the wounds?" Azrael asked. His eyes glistened with hope behind the mask he wore.

I weakly clenched my fist, but couldn't summon the strength to create my healing fire. "No." I lay limp with exhaustion and dropped onto the quilts. Perspiration dampened my clothes, but I could feel my temperature returning to normal.

Azrael tied a linen bandage around my arm. "You should get some rest." After making sure I was comfortable, he stood and headed for the cave's entrance.

"Azrael," I murmured. "Who is the key that will ignite Starfire?"

His lips turned up in a smile. His eyes glistened with delight as he bowed. "I am your key, Lady Aura."

Chapter Seven

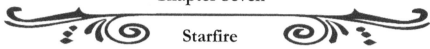

Starfire

I awoke in the dim cave. I didn't know how long I had slept after the treatment. My mind raced with a hundred emotions of excitement, but also doubt and suspicion. I brushed my hair back. I had been living in the human world for too long. Now I was suffering from culture shock after meeting my own kind.

I couldn't get my mind off what Azrael said about the power of Starfire. How could all the elements of creation exist inside me, a weak mortal? What if Azrael really was the key to unlocking my deep, repressed powers? That question frightened me more than my deadly gift. What did being my "key" mean?

I rolled over and patted the tiger sleeping next to me. Baby still had his eyes closed, but a low rumbling sound, almost like a purr, vibrated in his chest. I ran my fingers through his fur and kissed the big kitty on the nose. At least I hadn't out slept the cat.

I made my way to the cave entrance. The sun slowly dropped below the distant hills and painted the sky with the bold colors of a rainbow sunset.

"What're we going to do with her?" Orion asked.

The three men sat by the campfire. I could tell by their solemn expressions, I'd obviously walked in on a serious conversation. I stepped back into the cave and peered around the stone entrance.

Azrael shook his head. "We need to finish our mission and take her to the sanctuary. She'll be safe there."

"Maybe we should use her as bait," Korban suggested. "We can demolish another pack of Blood Hunters." He shoved his freshly sharpened blades into the scabbards on his back.

"She's not bait," Azrael scolded. "She's a lady, and the Lady of Neviah at that. Once she has rested, we need to finish our mission and make sure she's safe."

"She won't like it," Orion said in a teasing tone. "What if she puts up a fight?"

Korban laughed wildly. "She doesn't have a choice. Aura will come with us to the sanctuary one way or another."

"Are you suggesting we kidnap her?" Azrael asked, his tone now playful.

"If we must," Korban answered in a very business-like manner.

Orion crossed his arms over his burly chest. "She'll hate us for doing it."

Azrael shook his head and flashed a mischievous half smile. "She'll be thanking us later."

I had heard enough. I cleared my throat loud enough for them to hear. The three men jumped to their feet. Crimson guilt flooded each of their faces at my sudden appearance.

I walked toward them casually, as if I hadn't heard a word they said.

"Aura." Azrael kept his tone soft and passive, almost repentant. He offered me a seat next to him. "How are you feeling?"

The men waited chivalrously until I sat before they did. "Better." I folded my hands in my lap and didn't say another word. I reveled in the tension my silence caused as they tried to guess if I had heard their conversation. When I was done torturing them with my calm hush, I motioned toward my arm. "Thank you, Azrael. I know it wasn't easy for you."

Azrael gave me a soft smile.

I unraveled the bandage around my arm and assessed the wound. Hopefully, I had enough energy now to summon my elemental fire to heal myself. Korban eyed the wolf bite and leaned forward with morbid fascination. Orion's face went a shade whiter.

I balled my hand into a fist, letting the hot energy flow through me. My fingertips sizzled and glowed orange with heat before fire sprang to life and enveloped my arm. Azrael leaned away from me as the fire danced across my skin like oil on water. Muscle and tissue intertwined and reconnected until the cuts grew shallow and then closed. I released the flame and lowered my healed arm.

"Brilliant!" Korban cheered. "Can you heal other people?"

A teasing smile forced its way across my face. I arched one eyebrow and asked, "If you are ever wounded, do you want me to throw a ball of fire onto you and see what happens?"

Korban twisted his face into a grimace. Orion and Azrael laughed.

The sky darkened from lavender to indigo as the sun dipped further below the hills. Since I had slept all day, I doubt I would get any sleep tonight, especially after hearing their intentions to kidnap me. I debated whether I should escape after they fell asleep.

"Aura," Azrael started casually.

I jumped at the mention of my name. Korban eyed me. I was sure my involuntary reaction triggered his suspicion of my escape planning. I turned away from Korban and confidently met Azrael's gaze as I looked past the black mask over his brilliant eyes.

"Baby found something that we want to talk with you about," Azrael said.

"What is it?" I asked, wondering why Azrael sounded so concerned.

Azrael held up the bottle of poison Lucas gave me before I left London. "Do you know what this is?"

"Of course," I said nonchalantly. "It's poison. I was supposed to be an assassin after all."

Orion, who was usually silent when I was around, sputtered before forming his heavily accented words. "What imbecile told you that 'tis poison?"

"Lucas did." I narrowed my eyes at his insult. "He's the captain of the guard and my fiancé," I defended.

Azrael's teeth snapped together like I had hit him in the groin.

"That's not poison," Korban said, his eyes wide with intensity. "'Tis Shadow venom."

I shook my head in confusion. It couldn't be true.

Azrael handed me the bottle. "'Tis the same type of venom I pulled out of your arm. It attracts Shadow Lords and Blood Hunters to you."

I wrapped my fingers around the bottle. Why would Lucas have something like this? If he knew what it was, he would have never given it to me.

"Do you know where your . . . fiancé . . . got it?" Azrael asked. His voice sounded strained.

I shook my head. "I was just wondering the same thing myself."

"We need to get rid of it," Orion broke in, "before another pack of Blood Hunters pick up the scent."

I shivered from more than just the cold as the sky quickly grew dark. My stomach turned and I dropped the bottle of venom back into Azrael's waiting hand. He jumped to his feet then ran to the edge of our campsite near a small grove of trees. I couldn't help but smile at his masculine, energetic stride. Everything about him radiated valor and heroism. A brilliant fantasy of fighting the Shadow Legion alongside him sprang to my mind. I didn't know much about him, but I could tell he was someone I could count on in combat. He would be a great warrior to fight beside.

Azrael set the venom on the ground and took a few steps back. Fire shot from his hands. Gold light reflected off the leaves and lacy branches of the forest. The glass bottle rang like a banshee cry before it shattered.

Azrael looked back at me as if hoping for my approval. I smiled and nodded, even though I knew it would only feed his ego. It seemed that he and his cat had a lot in common.

Azrael strode toward me and grasped the bucket of venom-soaked rags. "Come with me." He held my hand and helped me to my feet. "I want you to see something." He took me to a small clearing away from camp, pulled out a rag spotted with just a few drops of my blood, and laid it on the ground.

He led me a few steps back before a stream of flames shot from his outstretched fingers. As soon as his elemental power touched my blood it erupted in a fire tsunami. The blast momentarily deafened my ears. My knees hit the ground. I covered my head with my hands. Azrael flung his cloak over me and stood as a buffer between me and the surge of energy flaming around us. Several nearby trees exploded. Splinters rained down on us like a thousand wooden daggers.

I turned my head and met Azrael's eyes, swirling with metallic shades of silver. "Was that Starfire?" I asked.

Azrael glanced over his shoulder at the blaze then helped me to my feet. "Yes, that intense power came from just a few drops of your blood."

A deep crater smoldered with white embers. Several holes marked the ground where the fire burned both the trees and roots. I swallowed hard and tried to grasp the amazing display of power and its significance.

Azrael stroked the top of my hand. White sparks skittered across my skin and lit our faces. His hot energy rushed through my arm where our hands joined. I couldn't look away from his intense eyes behind the mask. I kept my breath steady, but my heart pounded with apprehension. "If I am the fuel and you are the igniter," I said using his own analogy, "Should we stay away from each other?"

Azrael shook his head. "There is nothing in the universe that can keep me away from you now." His eyes filled with a passion that terrified me.

I pulled away from his touch. "Azrael, you shouldn't speak to me like that. I'm engaged." I looked at the stars to distract myself from him, but it didn't work. I could still feel him and his energy all around me. I pointed toward the camp and tried to sound indifferent. "Go back by the fire, and I will destroy the rest of the rags so you don't make a crater the size of Loch Lomond when your power touches my blood."

Azrael laughed, sounding too pleased with himself as he walked away.

I dumped the bucket of rags splattered in red blood and black venom to the ground. How could Azrael say that to me? I held out my hand and a stream of flames whirled from my fingers onto the rags. He knew I was engaged and his statement was obviously a romantic advance. The wet cloth sizzled then burned as it dried.

I thought about running away and never seeing him again, but with Starfire, he and I could defeat the whole Shadow Legion. Erebus wouldn't stand a chance against a power like ours.

I closed my eyes and let the heat flow from my body in waves. I couldn't run from Azrael. Despite my fears, we needed each other. I bit my lip. How would Lucas feel about him being around all the time, especially if Azrael was making advances?

"Maybe we should keep some of her blood," Korban said in hushed tones. I turned my head slightly to hear them better. "We can use her blood, combined with yours, and take down a castle wall."

"We are not Shadow Lords," Azrael said in a low, irritated voice. "We are not going to steal her blood."

Orion chuckled and nudged Azrael. "Besides, 'tis not Auriella's blood he wants to ignite."

Korban smiled smugly. "You've been looking for her all these years and when you finally find her, she's engaged." He tilted his head back in laughter. "Oh, the irony."

Azrael looked back at me. I quickly turned away. I heard him whispering, but I couldn't make out what he said.

I finished destroying the last of the rags and returned to the campfire. Azrael offered me a seat next to him, but I remained on my feet. "I need to talk to you men about something serious."

Korban and Orion looked at Azrael like he was about to be executed. Azrael froze like a statue of guilty ice.

"As you know, I was sent on a mission by the English king to assassinate the Scottish king, but I can't kill a human." I laced my hands together politely. "It's not our place as Watchers."

Orion and Korban both shifted nervously.

"No," Korban said. "Of course we wouldn't kill a human." His jaw tightened and his eyes darted from Azrael to Orion. Orion sputtered and Korban elbowed him in the ribs.

I had the distinct feeling they weren't jesting. I swallowed and continued, "I'm using this mission as an investigation to see if your king is a Shadow Lord in disguise. If he is human, perhaps I could negotiate an alliance between our countries."

"We have several Watchers at the castle in Edinburgh," Azrael assured.

I arched my eyebrow. "You have more than one?" I suddenly felt cheated that I had been on my own this whole time.

"We need more than one," Orion explained. "The Neviahan sanctuary 'tis on the Northern Isle, which makes Scotland a prime target for the Shadow Legion. The problem is the English." I flinched at his sour tone. "They keep attackin' us from the south, so we have to split our military forces."

"England isn't attacking you," I defended. "We are trying to help you. Don't you see? If we combine our kingdoms we will be strong enough to defeat the Shadow Legion—or, any other enemy for that matter."

Korban let out a quick, sarcastic laugh. "Is that what they told you? You have no idea what the English soldiers have put our people through."

"What are you talking about?" I asked. "King Edward wants peace."

"Is that why he sent you to assassinate our king?" Korban snapped.

I paused. What if they were right? "My king said it was your people who were attacking us." My voice sounded less sure.

"We are only defending ourselves," Korban said. "Scotland is a nation with a unique heritage, culture, and laws. We don't want another country's military patrolling our land. No man should be given too much power, especially not over other people lives."

I held up my hands and explained, "But England protects you from the invading countries of the south."

Korban's eyes narrowed. "And Scotland's people have been protecting England from the Vikings of the north."

Azrael, who had been unusually quiet this whole time, leaned back, crossed his legs, and put his hands behind his head. "England thinks they are protecting us? 'Tis not a fair assessment, since England starts most of its own wars."

The three Scotsmen laughed together.

"I don't think that's funny," I said through tight lips.

"I'm sorry, Lady Auriella," Azrael said. He leaned forward and gave me a playful half-smile. "It must be frustrating working for someone like King Edward."

I let out a gasp of surrender. He had no idea how little support I'd had since Edward took the throne. I kicked at the dirt. "Actually, it's more than frustrating—it's aggravating. He doesn't understand my position as a Watcher."

Korban smirked. "We figured as much if he sent you on an assassination mission." He dropped another log on the fire. Red ash floated into the air, contrasting the white stars above.

The firelight danced across Korban's intense, chiseled features as he continued, "Our spies in the Middle East have watched Erebus's movements for years. We tracked him all the way to London. We had no doubt the Shadow King was after you." He motioned toward me. "We believe he found information on you through the crusaders."

Orion's face wrinkled in puzzlement. "Why do the English keep sending crusaders to the Middle East?" he asked me. "Don't they know about the curse?"

I shook my head. "What curse?"

"You don't know about the curse?" Korban's eyes went wide with disbelief. "No one can rule or govern the Middle East. Those who live there will be in a constant state of war until the end of the world."

Orion laughed at Korban. "You can be so dramatic."

I crossed my arms and wondered if they were just trying to scare me.

Azrael turned to me and got to the point of their story. "We thought you could use some help defending the castle in London, since you are the only Watcher in England." I was about to agree when he stopped me. "But—now that you're here, we're going to take you to the safety of the Neviahan sanctuary. After that, we will go after Erebus ourselves."

Korban and Orion cheered at the battle announcement. "Huzzah!"

"You're not fighting Erebus without me." I narrowed my eyes and dared any of them to stop me.

"'Tis not up for debate, my lady." Azrael leaned back and looked at the night sky. "You don't know how Erebus works. He's killed dozens of Watchers and stolen their powers. Fighting him is like fighting a small army with super powers. His tactics are subtle webs of complex traps. By the time you know you're in danger, 'tis too late. Our mission is to get you safely to the sanctuary," Azrael explained. "You made things easy for us, since we didn't have to travel all the way to London."

"Yeah," Korban said. "You practically fell onto our shields."

Azrael threw him a warning glare.

I flexed my jaw and took in a quick breath. "And what about my mission?"

Korban let out a low sarcastic laugh. "You're going to assassinate our king?"

I pressed my lips tight. "No, I want to be a diplomat between our two countries. Humans should not be fighting against each other when there's a bigger battle at hand. If we can bring peace between Scotland and England, then we can combine our forces to defeat the Shadow Legion." I looked at each of the men, waiting for their approval of my idea.

Azrael stared at the fire in front of us. Korban crossed his arms and looked like he was about to laugh. Orion seemed more interested in the ground than in me. I dropped my shoulders, but I wouldn't be defeated. "Help me destroy Erebus and I will go willingly to the sanctuary," I bargained.

Azrael's head snapped up. His eyes searched mine with interest as if debating whether he should accept my offer. I knew he wanted me to go with him, but I needed to know that my country was safe before I left. As much as I hated to admit it, I needed their help too.

Korban kept his stern composure and said, "We need reinforcements to take back London. Do you really think that just the four of us can defeat Erebus and his army?"

"We have Starfire," I reminded, and I flashed them a confident smile. "I'm not afraid to use it."

Azrael's eyes beamed with excitement. His whole body radiated white energy. I was sure he would take the bait now and convince the others to come to London.

I turned back to Korban. "You even said so yourself—we can take down a castle wall with just a few drops of my blood. If Azrael and I combine our powers, just think of what we can do to Erebus and his army."

Korban paused, then stroked his chin. He gazed away in deep thought. Orion stared at the fire, his brow creased.

Azrael finally broke the silence. "The only way we could win would be to use Starfire." He stood and stepped toward me. "Are you sure about this?" he whispered.

I took a deep breath. "I'm sure." My gaze didn't waver as I stared into his eyes behind his dark mask.

His voice sounded confident and pleased. "This will be the first time Starfire has been used against the Rebellion in over a thousand years." One corner of his perfect mouth lifted. "You and I will create one amazing light show in London."

Chapter Eight

Scottish King

I dug through my saddle bag, which thankfully survived the fire fight, and pulled out my brocade slippers. They weren't riding boots, but they would have to do until I got back to London. I retrieved the dress I carefully selected to wear before the Scottish king and shook out the wrinkles.

I still wasn't sure what to say to the king. Just because I wanted peace didn't mean the two monarchs of England and Scotland would. I pursed my lips with irritation. It seems the only people who enjoy war are kings who don't fight in battle themselves.

I was more worried about what to say to Lucas when I returned to London than what to say to the barbarian king. I had lost my engagement ring, but more pressing, how would Lucas feel about leaving London and coming to the sanctuary with me and the other Neviahans? How would he feel about Azrael and our intimate Starfire connection?

Lucas was a good human, a knight for his country, and a friend. Azrael, well, he was barbaric, abrupt, and forward. I'm sure his terrifying traits had to do something with being raised by the Scottish.

I folded my dress and placed it back into the saddle bag before examining my horse's injuries. Whatever salve Azrael had used to heal my horse worked well. I ran my finger over her smooth scars.

I stood up and whirled into Azrael, his nose inches away from mine. "Azrael!" I breathed and stepped away. I had no idea how long he had been standing behind me. "You scared me."

Azrael laughed playfully. I put my hands on my hips and gave him a stern glare as I tried not to laugh myself.

"We are ready to leave," he informed me.

I stroked my horse's nose. "Are you sure she is ready to ride?" I motioned toward the scars.

Azrael nodded, but added, "Now, I wouldn't let a big man like Orion ride her, but she will get you to Edinburgh and back to London."

I glanced at Orion, who looked too big to ride even his own massive shire horse.

"Do you need assistance mounting?" Azrael asked me. By his wide smile, I could tell he was too eager to put his hands around my waist.

I furrowed my brow. "No!" I said louder than I should have. I didn't feel sorry about it either. He was trying to make advances. If Lucas were here I had no doubt he would have challenged Azrael to a duel. "I can manage." I turned my back to him as I gripped the saddle and swung my leg over the horse.

Azrael held up the reins. I took them, and he intentionally let his hand linger over mine a little too long. I glanced away and pretended I hadn't noticed.

Azrael turned from me and mounted his horse. "Are you ready?"

I nodded, but refused to speak to him. I had met men like him before—too confident for their own good. I would have to set boundaries in our "fuel and igniter" relationship, not only for him, but for myself too. He was the kind of man every woman fell in love with. I wasn't going to fall into that trap.

He looked back and flashed me a perfect smile. His eyes shone out through the black mask as if it weren't there. I clenched my teeth and forced myself not to smile back.

Baby bounced along the trail and then back to the group as if he was irritated we weren't as fast as him. Azrael rode beside me, Orion rode behind, and Korban in front. They formed a shield around me as if worried we might run into Erebus himself on the foreign road. All three stayed vigilant and watched the woods. Even Baby occasionally stopped and sniffed the air before pressing forward.

I hadn't brought a map, and the Scottish roads were obscurely marked—if there were any markers at all. "How many days travel to

Edinburgh?" I intentionally asked Orion the question instead of Azrael.

"Well," Orion said, dragging out his voice. "Since we 'ave you with us, it'll take twice as long. I'd say two or three days."

"I travel well," I assured him and tried not to sound offended that he thought I would slow them down. "I'm not as delicate as you think."

Korban let out a burst of laughter. "You have no idea how delicate and vulnerable you are."

King Edward had said something similar to me before I left. I let out a sigh. Neviahan and human men were all the same.

"Do you want to travel through the night?" Azrael asked. His tone indicated a challenge.

Korban looked over his shoulder and shook his head.

"She's going to fall off her horse," Orion said.

Perhaps if I traveled through the night, they would see I wasn't delicate. I sat a little taller. "I can do it." Besides, I had gotten more than enough sleep in the last twenty-four hours after Azrael drained the venom from my arm.

"Azrael!" Korban shouted. "Why did you challenge her?"

Azrael laughed and glanced at me. "Because I knew she couldn't resist." I narrowed my eyes. He had tricked me. Azrael looked away and said casually, "Besides, she's worried about her fiancé. The sooner she talks with the king, the sooner she can return to London." Azrael didn't face me.

The sun glowed like a white orb through the clouds over head. My energy seemed to wane on overcast days like this, but at least it kept my Lifelight from sparkling and distracting everyone.

In my mind, I went over speeches of diplomacy for the King of Scotland. Their culture was so different from what I knew in London. Azrael's plaid kilt wrapped around his loins like a short skirt. His bare legs hung down over his unsaddled horse. I could only imagine how sore he would be after riding all day and all night. I smiled to myself. He would see. I would outlast him in this challenge of riding through the night.

Korban pulled his horse off the road toward a stream. If they planned on taking a break every few hours, this would be easy. Azrael, Orion, and I followed Korban to the stream. Moss covered the streambed and rowan trees.

Azrael bounded from his horse with ease and reached out to take my hand. I looked away and dismounted as I had done thousands of times without his chivalrous aid. My feet hit the wet grass surrounding the stream and slipped out from under me. I wasn't used to wearing the brocade slippers outdoors. If that wasn't embarrassing enough, Azrael had the nerve to reach out with inhuman speed and snatch me before I hit the ground.

My face flushed. I shrugged away from him.

"You're welcome," he said even though I hadn't thanked him. I didn't turn to look at him, but I knew he was smiling. I took deep breaths to calm my nerves.

I retrieved my canteen from the saddle bag and filled it after I let my hands linger in the cold water as a feeble effort to stop his energy from racing through me. It happened every time he touched me. My hands grew cold, but the rest of my body burned vehemently. I put the canteen to my lips, hoping the water would chill the fiery spirit inside me.

"Don't push her," Korban said under his breath to Azrael.

"I know what I'm doing," Azrael whispered. "Trust me."

I put the cork back over the opening of my canteen. They were planning something. Azrael knew more about me and my powers than he let on.

I stayed vigilant as I walked on the slick wet moss and mounted my horse. I pulled on the reins and faced Edinburgh. The sooner we got there, the better. "Do you boys need to rest longer?" I asked in a taunting tone.

Korban threw his leg over his horse and mounted. Azrael and Orion mounted their horses as well. Baby finished lapping up a drink then he too, fell in line.

Eventually, the woods gave way to rolling hills of jade hues. The overcast sky seemed to intensify the wet green landscape. I took a deep breath of cool country air as the wind tangled through my hair like a lover's gentle fingers. The horses' hooves hit the earth in a lullaby rhythm. I still hadn't thought of what to say to the king of Scotland—or Lucas, for that matter.

There is always a better solution than war. I just had to make everyone see it. The sky grew darker and the world colder. The warmth of the sun faded on my back as we continued east. I gripped my cloak tighter and sat taller to defy the sleep creeping over me. The fight with the Blood Hunters and healing my wounded arm had used more energy than I expected. I yawned.

Azrael glanced at me.

I forced my yawn back, brightened my eyes, and smiled. I wasn't going to fall asleep and let him win.

"She's going to fall off her horse," Orion muttered again.

I ignored him. I had enough on my mind to keep me awake. I hoped the Scottish king would be reasonable in his requests of King Edward. What if the Scots leased their army to the English for a fee? That way both kingdoms would be satisfied. The Scots would get income and Edward would get his army.

The overcast sky hid the stars and made the world pitch black. The tiger's eyes glinted in the deep night. A second set of reflective eyes watched the woods. I squinted to make sure I wasn't seeing things. "Azrael?"

Azrael whirled around at the mention of his name. His eyes flashed like silver moonlight.

"Your eyes," I gasped.

His eyes narrowed as he smiled. "Night vision," he answered. "When Watchers get their animal companions we take on some of their attributes."

"Astonishing," I said. I relaxed a little and leaned over my saddle. At least there would be no surprise attacks. Baby and Azrael wouldn't let anything happen.

I went back to my dilemma of what to say when I met with the Scottish king. I thought about how to do my hair, since there was only one option of what to wear. I imagined my formal wardrobe at home in London. I loved the way my long, heavy skirts sounded as I danced around the ballroom. I imagined Lucas in his crusader tunic. He smiled and looked deep into my eyes. I leaned into him as we danced.

Lucas's mouth opened wide, his pupils narrowed to a snake-like slit. I screamed and tried to jerk away as he coiled around me. Lucas's devouring jaw unlocked from the rest of his skull. "No!" I fought to free myself from his suffocating grip.

My eyes sprang open. The light of the morning momentarily blinded me. I gripped the arms wrapped around me and tried to fight the feeling of the serpent's coil.

"Easy," Azrael whispered. His deep eyes stared down at me as he held me in his arms. I blinked, not breaking away from his eternally deep gaze. I put my hand to my forehead and brushed back my hair. "I fell asleep," I realized out loud.

Azrael wrapped his arms victoriously around me. "I caught you before you hit the ground."

This was a disaster. I wanted to run away in shame and hide. I was angry at myself and furious at Azrael. I never wanted to see him again. I just wanted to get home to Lucas where I belonged.

Korban still rode in front and Orion rode behind with my vacant horse walking beside him. Orion grinned wide as if to say, 'I knew you would fall off your horse.'

I covered my face and shook my head. This was officially the most embarrassing moment of my life. I should have never pushed myself when I needed to rest.

I stared at the dewy Scottish hills and didn't say anything to Azrael. I didn't know what to say.

I sat stiff in his arms and tried not to jump every time his hot skin brushed across mine. I swallowed the awkward lump knotting in my throat. I had to say something. The silence only added to the tension of the moment. He probably had no idea how riding in his arms made me feel. The warmth of his body close to mine frightened me.

Was it dangerous for us to be this close to each other? Images of the fiery crater flashed through my mind. Azrael knew more about Starfire than I did, and yet his arms seemed relaxed wrapped around me. His strong hands calmly held the reins. He wouldn't be holding me this way if he was afraid I would combust into flames and kill every living thing within a hundred leagues.

I tried to read his expression for a hint of what he was thinking. The mask hid too much for me to read his face at this angle.

"Why do you wear that mask?" I finally asked. I tried to sound casual. After all, I had no reason to feel nervous.

"This?" Azrael reached up and touched his mask. "'Tis a curse of mine."

"Curse?" My eyes widened at the intriguing mystery. I could tell there was a great story behind why he wore the mask.

"From a quest many years ago. I didn't exactly fail, but I didn't succeed either." He laughed to himself.

"Can you tell me what happened?" I asked, and then looked down at my hands. "That is, if you want to talk about it."

Azrael gave me a soft smile. "Anything you want to know about me I will tell you. I won't ever keep secrets from you. I want you to know me, flaws and all."

I didn't deserve that kind of trust from him, especially since I intentionally gave him the cold shoulder more than once.

"A long time ago, I was sent on a series of druid missions," Azrael started. "On one of these missions I captured a Shadow Lord named Molech. I should have killed him, but I didn't. I kept him alive to try and get information about Erebus, the Shadow King. Unfortunately, Molech knew my weakness."

"What is your weakness?" I asked. Usually I didn't ask such personal questions, but it was hard to imagine Azrael having any weakness at all.

"Pride," Azrael said. "I was too proud. That led to a temporary downfall . . . a very dark downfall," he emphasized. "Molech fed my ego and one day I decided I didn't need to follow the Druids of Neviah anymore, so I joined the Shadow Legion for a time."

I gasped. "The Shadow Legion?" I couldn't imagine why any Watcher would turn against their own king and fall.

"Even though I'm fighting for the Kingdom of Neviah again, I must wear this until the curse is broken." He pointed to the mask. "I must wear it for a long time." His intense gaze flashed to mine. "But I have faith that one day the curse will be broken."

"What do you have to do to break the curse?" I asked. It sounded like an epic adventure in the making and I wanted in on the challenge.

Azrael paused as if choosing his words carefully. "The woman I love, must love me in return."

The wind escaped my lungs, and I looked away from his powerful eyes. I couldn't help but feel he thought I was the one to break his curse.

I shook off the feeling and pretended not to take his hint. "I've been prideful too," I admitted. Azrael tilted his head like he didn't understand. I explained, "Because of my pride I pushed myself too hard, fell asleep, and then fell off my horse." I had no idea how Azrael was able to dismount his own horse so quickly and catch me, but I was grateful he had. The last thing I needed was to return to London injured. Everyone, including Lucas, would blame the Scottish, and my mission for peace would be devastated. I forced myself to look into his brilliant dark eyes. "Thank you for saving me—again."

Azrael looked startled by my acceptance of his chivalry. His perfect mouth twitched into a soft smile. "'Twas my pleasure."

I looked away and pressed my lips tight. I could only imagine his pleasure at having me ride in his barbaric arms—his bare arms—his strong, battle-sculpted warrior arms. Perfect skin wrapped around his granite muscles. He must have fought in many battles. Tight veins of fiery blood lined his forearms. Heat rose to my face. I looked away to break the trance. "I don't usually fall off my horse," I assured. "I can take care of myself."

"Of course," Azrael quickly agreed. "But I will always be there to catch you."

I had the feeling he was just trying to appease me while cleaving to his victory. "I don't need saving." I kept my voice hard.

"Your eyes are green," he noted.

"No, they're hazel," I corrected. "Except when I'm using my powers—then they're gold."

Azrael laughed and shook his head. "No, they are definitely green. The brightest shade I've ever seen." Azrael had no reason to lie to me.

"Green? Why would my eyes suddenly turn green?"

His arms involuntarily flexed around me when he shrugged.

I pulled my hair over my shoulder and picked at the stray ends to distract myself.

Azrael stiffened as if I slapped him when my hair brushed along his skin. His hands gripped the reins tighter. He stopped breathing, but I could feel his heart pounding like a Celtic war drum in his chest.

I leaned away. Had I done something wrong?

I counted the seconds I didn't feel him breathe.

Korban called from up ahead. "There, 'tis Edinburgh."

Edinburgh Castle dominated the skyline on a volcanic mountain surrounded by a lush valley. Moss and vines garnished the dark rock like a pillar of pride. The construction wasn't of delicate arches and spiraling towers as I had expected to see. The sturdy castle looked as immovable as the mountain itself. I felt sorry for any army who tried to lay siege on such a fortress.

My stomach fluttered with doubt and excitement as we rode through the gate into the inner castle wall. Everyone seemed to know the three Neviahan warriors and didn't question that I was with them.

No squires rushed forward to help us dismount, but instead Azrael, Korban, and Orion led their own horses into the stable.

I allowed Azrael to take my waist and help me from the saddle. I didn't need his help, but I allowed him to be a gentleman.

"I know this isn't London," Azrael said, "but we will try to make you feel at home."

"I won't be here long," I reminded. "My people in London need me just as much as your people need you here in Edinburgh."

"Remember who our real people are. Remember where our real kingdom is." Azrael pointed at the sky.

I lost myself in his eyes. Azrael and I were the same. The Great Kingdom of Neviah was our kingdom, and this war wasn't about north versus south or progress versus tradition. Our war was light against darkness. Somehow, I had to convince the humans to stop fighting each other and focus on defeating the Shadow Legion.

A deep voice came from behind. "My lords." A middle-aged man wearing a tunic trimmed in sheepskin bowed. "The king and lords await your report. They expected you back days ago." He looked around Orion's bulky frame and eyed me.

Korban brushed past Azrael and whispered under his breath, "The king isn't going to be happy about her."

Orion and Korban glanced away from me. I met Azrael's eyes. "What does he mean?" I didn't hide my concern.

Azrael shook his head. "You're right where you should be, so don't worry."

The castle hallways seemed to pass in a blur as Azrael, Korban, and Orion led me toward the king's court. The knot in my stomach tightened. My hands grew slick with perspiration and I brushed them on my skirt. I thought I would have a little more time when we arrived to prepare my speech for the king. As it was, I didn't even have time to make myself look presentable.

Azrael put his arm around my shoulders and pulled me close. "You'll do fine. How could anyone not love everything about you?"

"I think you might be biased," I murmured. My eyes darted around the hall as I memorized the layout just in case I needed to make a quick escape.

Azrael tilted his head back and let out a deep laugh. His voice echoed off the walls. "You are a Neviahan woman, and the Lady of Neviah at that. You have no idea how much power you have, even as a mortal."

"I look awful, Azrael." I motioned toward my travel clothes. One sleeve was torn where the wolf had bitten me. My scarlet brocade shoes didn't match the earth-toned dress. My skirt was intentionally split in several places to make riding easier, and it was obvious that I wore tight doe-skin riding breaches underneath.

Azrael assessed me. His eyes filled with satisfaction. "You look stunning. I've never seen a woman like you before."

I waved his compliment away. Of course he hadn't ever seen a woman like me. I was a disaster.

"You will find that King Alexander of Scotland respects warriors not for their land, beauty, or clothing, but for their confidence, character, and courage." Azrael leaned toward me and whispered in my ear, "Four Shadow Wolves."

I laughed. My fears melted as I thought about my victory. "That's a new record for me."

"'Tis impressive," Azrael agreed. "Those weren't pups, either. We thought you weren't going to leave any Blood Hunters for us to kill."

I met his gaze and didn't hold back the smile pressing across my face. Azrael beamed back. His expression of joy shone clear and genuine as if he weren't even wearing that ridiculous cursed mask.

We passed through the doorway into the great hall. For some reason, I had imagined a simple meeting with the king over a cup of tea. I wasn't expecting this.

Lords and warriors of high station filled the room. Smoke lingered from the fire pits. The sunlight streamed weakly through the windows and shone off the smoke, making it look like solid white beams. I could feel a hundred pairs of eyes watching me.

The Celtic barbarian lords were dressed in kilts and battle tunics. Some of them were painted with a misty blue hue down their faces and across their bare chests. Everyone was armed, and not with fancy show weapons like the men of the English courts, but with crude axes and worn blades. Their weapons seemed to be part of who they were. I had the distinct feeling that the men of this court were all battle-seasoned veterans.

Four Shadow Wolves, I reminded myself to be brave.

Korban and Orion strode to the throne and knelt. Azrael knelt too. I swallowed hard and gracefully curtsied. The king seemed surprised by my gesture. I'm sure he noticed the leather breaches under my split skirt.

"Arise," King Alexander said. He waited until all were on their feet before leaning forward and asking informally, "Did you find the assassin?"

My tongue tightened. I clenched my skirt in my fists. I knew he was talking about me.

"Yes," Korban said. "We found the assassin."

My blood ran cold. I could feel it in my trembling hands. I glanced at Azrael with pleading eyes. He kept his business-like gaze straight ahead of him.

Korban gestured to me. I froze in place. "There were nine of them. England's Watcher destroyed four of them before we arrived. She saved the life of a Scotsman in Gretna as well."

I unclenched my hands, relieved they weren't calling me out.

King Alexander met my gaze. His expression wasn't judgmental, but full of wonder. "This is England's Watcher?"

Murmurs of disbelief echoed from the lords in the room.

"I'm surprised at you, Azrael," King Alexander said, "You are the mightiest warrior in battle and fight like a dragon. I thought you would choose a warrior who is more your equal to be your war companion. I have a hard time believing this lass is the warrior who can take out a field of soldiers?"

Azrael's jaw tightened. "With all due respect, you of all people know that strength is not measured by the number of armies we defeat. Strength is measured by how we survive and stand back up to keep fighting."

King Alexander leaned back. His massive hands gripped the arms of his rugged throne of distressed wood. He finally spoke to me. "You must be very brave, for coming into enemy territory. You also must be very strong to be the only Watcher in England." The king stroked his beard. "Tell me, why would an English woman want to travel a long, dangerous road, rescuing people who are not her responsibility to save?"

My first thought was, why wouldn't I save humans? I'm a Watcher, and it's my duty. I kept my shoulders square and my voice steady. "For peace. I hope our two countries can come to an understanding, Your Highness."

Alexander's eyes glistened with a mixture of fury and respect. "As noble as you are, my lady, I want your king and his armies out of my kingdom. That is the only way we will have peace."

"We can help each other," I said. "I'm sure King Edward would be willing to give you whatever you ask in exchange for your aid."

King Alexander jumped off his throne and strode toward me with a furious stride. His chainmail clanked and his boots pounded against the stone floor.

I should have been terrified, but I was more awestruck at his powerful presence. King Alexander's armor was worn and battle-beaten. I noted a few places where the armor had been repaired with leather and metal straps. This wasn't anything like the fancy, polished armor Edward wore for display.

Alexander marched closer. Azrael stiffened. The tendons in his forearms strained across his flexed muscles.

Alexander froze in place, looked at Azrael, then back at me. "Tell your king that what I want is for his armies to leave my kingdom. We are not the invaders! Your soldiers have come onto my lands, killed my people, raped our women, and taken whatever they pleased."

I swallowed hard. It couldn't be true. Why would humans do such horrible things to each other? Rebels must be behind these horrendous acts.

The king continued, "It doesn't matter how much that coward of a king pays us—we will not give him more military aid. If we did, he would still unlawfully tax us while our men do all the fighting and dying in Edward's battles." Alexander sucked in a deep breath and turned away from me.

"What about the Shadow Legion?" I asked. "They are the ones we should be fighting."

The king spun toward me. "You're right, my lady. But right now, the demons we must fight are the ones Edward—not Erebus—sends to destroy us. Perhaps one day we can join the Watchers in your effort to defeat the Shadow Legion. As of now, when human history is told, people will speak of the how the Scottish fought valiantly against the English for their independence."

I pushed back my own disappointments. "Your Majesty," I addressed him. "I know you will be victorious." I noted his worn armor again and wished I could work for such a leader. "You have more strength of character than any king I've ever met. I will gladly take your message back to Edward and fight for your cause in London."

Alexander blinked away a stunned expression. His lips momentarily turned up in a smile. "I misjudged you. Forgive me, my lady." He stayed regal, though his voice was thoughtful. "I see a rare strength in you. You seem disconnected from this world in a way only a valiant warrior with an eternal perspective on life can be disconnected. Your cares are not of the world, but for the people in it."

King Alexander brushed past Azrael and whispered something just loud enough for him to hear.

Azrael grinned and replied, "Yes, Your Majesty. 'Tis a promise."

Chapter Nine

 Starfire Accident

Though it was morning, dark clouds covered the sky, making everything seem gloomy. Rain drizzled down and splashed off the stone frame of the glassless window. I wrapped my shawl tighter around my shoulders. I could taste the dampness in the breeze blowing down the hallway. Every bitter step on the stone floor chilled my feet.

I couldn't help but feel discouraged about my mission, and curious about the last secret words the Scottish king had said to Azrael.

Footsteps softly pounded against the stone floor behind me. I didn't turn around. I knew it was Azrael by the way my energy level spiked. He stood beside me and we just stared out the window together.

"I bet the peasants in their homes below look up at the castle and wish they could live in this majestic fortress," Azrael said. "And yet, those in this cold, airy castle look down on the warm, cozy cottages with envy. 'Tis a very human trait to want something you don't have and not appreciate what you do have."

"There have been many times I have felt so human," I admitted.

Azrael nodded in understanding, "We all feel human at times, but we have to remember we are not them. We are their Watchers."

It was true. I couldn't get caught up in human problems and emotions. I had work to do. "Azrael, I have to return to London. Erebus will be there any day."

Azrael's eyes focused out the window on the misty road winding though the valley toward the dense forest. "Going to London is the same as going to war. Do you understand the risk?"

I swallowed hard and answered with a nod.

"You don't have to go," Azrael said. "We could take you to the sanctuary, then Orion, Korban and I will return to London with a full army."

He was just trying to protect me. "Azrael, I need to go. With all the hate between our countries, what will the English think when they see an army led by three Scotsmen riding into London? They won't think you are there to fight Erebus. It will be a blood bath on both sides. I must lead you there in order to avoid this."

Azrael let out a surrendering sigh as if he knew I was right. "Then we will pack light to make better speed to London."

Within the hour we mounted our horses and the northern wind pushed against our backs as if urging us forward.

My energy waned under the sunless sky. Korban was in front while Orion stayed in the rear of our tiny four person army. Azrael rode beside me. Raindrops fell through the trees, creating dark spots on our wool cloaks.

I had no idea what to expect when I returned home, except that King Edward would be furious, Lucas would be happy to see me, and we would be hopelessly outnumbered against Erebus's armies.

I hadn't discovered any useful information for Edward, and I hadn't assassinated anyone either. In fact, I discovered my own people were the true enemies of Scottish peace. Edward wouldn't listen to me, but Lucas would. I could always count on him. Once I explained the situation to Lucas, he would petition to the king on my behalf.

Azrael's gentle voice interrupted my thoughts. "Don't be disappointed. Despite what King Edward will say, your mission to Scotland was successful."

"We will see," I mused. "I wish there was more I could have done. Peace seems hopeless."

Azrael reached across the gap between us and held my hand. "In war, there is always hope, and there is always light." He pulled away and gripped his reins. I could still feel the warmth of his hand on mine, even after he let go.

The horses' hooves sloshed on the road, engraved with horse and cart tracks. The journey back to London was going to be one of the longest weeks of my life.

I shook my head, trying to shake the worry from my mind. I couldn't give up. "You're right, Azrael. I just hope I will be received well when I return to London."

"I'm sure your fiancé will be thrilled when you return safely." There was no bitterness in his voice.

I looked away as new worry crept into my mind. Once I got back, I had to find out why Lucas had the Shadow venom. If he knew what it was, he would never have sent it with me. Images of the Shadow Wolves pacing the river's edge flashed across my mind. My stomach tightened into a sick knot. At least Azrael had been there to pull me from the water and—I stopped in mid-thought and imagined Azrael's perfect lips over mine as he breathed into my lungs and forced out the river water.

Azrael turned and smiled at me with those perfect lips. My face flared like a bonfire bursting to life. I turned away. My warm, uneven breath hit the cold air. I scolded myself for feeling this way.

The road became muddier and we slowed our pace.

Baby walked ahead of Korban as if he led the tiny caravan. His eyes narrowed and his nose wrinkled in disgust as he tiptoed along the grassy edge of the road to avoid the mud.

"A big kitten like you, 'tis afraid to get his feet dirty?" Azrael teased.

Baby let out a hiss. My grip tightened on the reins of my startled horse.

Azrael bellowed a warm baritone laugh.

"It's like he can understand you." I had seen people talk with the cats before, but the conversation was mostly one sided as they answered their cat's meow with, "Yes, yes, I know."

"He can," Azrael admitted, but the way he smiled made me wonder if he was teasing. "And I can understand him," he continued in a more serious tone. "All Neviahans have the ability to communicate with their animal companions."

"Like, full conversations?" I asked and purposefully looked back at Orion to validate what Azrael had said.

Orion shrugged his massive shoulders, "'Tis true."

I still couldn't believe it. "Do you have an animal companion?" I asked Orion.

"'Tis a worm," Azrael said. He couldn't hold a straight face.

Orion threw Azrael a dark glare, but his expression softened before answering me, "I haven't gotten my animal companion yet. What about you?"

I shook my head. "No, I don't have one either." Now that I knew I could have a pet I could talk to, I really wanted one. "Will I get my animal companion at the sanctuary?"

"Not necessarily," Azrael said. "When the time is right, your animal companion will find you."

The rain no longer fell in drops from the sky, but turned into a fine, wet mist around us.

"What kind of companion will I have?" I hoped it wouldn't be a snake or rat.

Azrael shrugged. "You won't know until one day, an animal walks up to you and starts talking."

"Can Baby understand me?" I asked.

Azrael answered with a nod.

I tried to recall everything I'd ever said to Baby and hoped I hadn't embarrassed myself by sharing anything too personal. "Can he talk to me?"

"No, but he keeps trying to," Azrael answered.

"What does he say?" My curiosity piqued.

Azrael's eyes twinkled with laughter. "Most of the time he says things inappropriate for a lady to hear. 'Tis a good thing you can't understand him."

"Oh," I replied and felt myself blush again.

"You haven't been telling him any secrets, have you?" Korban asked. "'Cause that cat blabs everything."

I narrowed my eyes. "I'm not the one with secrets." I turned and looked at Azrael as if trying to pierce his soul with my gaze.

Azrael held up his hands in a surrendering gesture. "I told you I would tell you everything you want to know about me."

"What did the king tell you before we left Edinburg?"

Azrael grinned and held me with his captivating eyes. His voice dropped to a gentle whisper. "He said you are a fine woman and I should always respect you as an equal."

I broke free from his enchanting gaze and let my hair fall forward like a scarlet curtain between us. The only way to defeat Erebus would be to use Starfire. "People are counting on us. I need to know everything about Erebus so I can be prepared in battle."

Azrael still smiled, but I forced my lips into a tight line. I was proud of myself for staying regal while he kept trying to break my defenses. It was easy to be serious when I talked about war and Erebus.

"What do you know about the war in the Kingdom of Neviah?" Azrael asked. All teasing tones and flirtatiousness left him as he sat a little straighter.

I shrugged. "Hardly anything. Only that one-third of the kingdom rebelled and we are still fighting that war here on Earth."

Azrael nodded. "The Great King of Neviah had seven sons. They each controlled one of the seven major elements: Spirit, Life, Death, Wind, Fire, Earth, and Water. Erebus was one of the seven princes."

"Erebus?" I couldn't believe it. Was Azrael talking about the same rebel who was trying to cause the complete destruction of the human race? Erebus couldn't possibly be a prince of Neviah. "Why would Erebus turn against his own kingdom?"

"'Twas because of the first son's decision. The first prince was destined to inherit all that his father had—the whole kingdom. Do you know how many stars and planets that is?" Azrael didn't wait for me to guess. "The first son wanted to share it with every Neviahan. That way, we would all be heirs to endless worlds and kingdoms."

I held up my hand, stopping him from going on until I asked, "So the first son, to whom the throne rightfully belonged, wanted to create a democracy and do away with the monarchy?"

"Sort of," Azrael answered. "This isn't like any political endeavor Earth has ever known. All members of Neviah would be kings and queens as they became joint heirs with the first son." I tried to imagine what it would be like if a prince of England did something like that. Azrael continued, "The second son, Erebus, wanted to keep all the king's power and glory for himself."

I lifted my gaze from the road and pursed my lips as if pushing a sour taste from my mouth. "Power seems to be a common theme with the Shadow Legion." I couldn't help it, my words still sounded bitter.

Azrael had his war face on. His eyes focused on the road ahead of us and his voice lowered. "Erebus gathered followers to overthrow the king and eldest son. After the first Neviahan war, the rebels stripped themselves of light and searched for new power in the darkness." He turned to look at me, his eyes were fierce and a thrill ran through me. "That's when they came to Earth. Now, Erebus is trying to start his own kingdom with himself as the king here on Earth. And because they have no natural Neviahan power anymore, they hunt us Watchers for our power."

I shook my head to break away from his intense gaze. Erebus wanted this world to be his own dark Neviah. I knew that meant he wanted to initiate a holocaust and the complete genocide of the human race.

Orion's deep voice came from behind. "We cast them out once before—we can do it again!"

"Huzzah!" Korban cheered in agreement.

I couldn't help but smile at their unconquerable enthusiasm.

Azrael continued, "The only problem is that our numbers are fewer on Earth. As you saw yesterday in the meeting with the king, the humans aren't going to be much help."

The war on Earth was more complicated than I had imagined. "How many other Neviahans are here on Earth?" I asked.

"Tens of thousands," Azrael answered.

I jumped with surprise and gripped my saddle to keep from falling off. I sheepishly glanced over my shoulder at Orion, who always seemed to predict I would fall off my horse.

Orion shook his head.

I turned back to Azrael. "I had no idea there were so many of us. You three are the first I've ever met."

Azrael rode a little closer. "You will meet a whole lot more once we make it to the sanctuary."

I looked away. After we took care of the problems in London I would have to keep my promise and go to the sanctuary. Things were going to change for me, but was it really a good idea for me to leave the people I'm supposed to protect? Perhaps I made the promise too hastily.

"What is it?" Azrael asked. He had a way of sensing my emotions as if he felt them himself.

I stuttered as if choking on my words. "Will Lucas be able to come with me to the sanctuary?" I was still torn in so many ways about Lucas. I really did care for him and it would tear him apart if I had to leave him after we had just been reunited.

"The Neviahans have strict rules about humans and Watchers intermixing," Azrael said in a firm tone, but he seemed to pull away as if he didn't want to talk about it.

"What do you mean?" I prodded. I wasn't going to let him retreat that easily. "We work with humans all the time."

Azrael didn't say anything. I stared at him, not giving up until I got an answer.

Orion broke the silence, "Intermarriage is forbidden."

"What? Why?" I suddenly felt condemned. I couldn't marry who I wanted to? I looked to where my engagement ring should be on my hand. My heart sank.

Just when I thought it couldn't get any worse Korban said, "If you bore a child, then we would have to kill it. The Nephilim are against the laws of nature."

Horror rushed over me. How could they kill an innocent baby? This all sounded so terrible.

"Stop," Azrael said in the sharpest tone I had ever heard him use. "Auriella can marry whomever she wishes." I still didn't look at him. For some reason I felt ashamed now. Korban threw Azrael a warning glare. Azrael ignored the warning and continued, "If her fiancé has any brains or balls, he will follow her to the ends of the Earth."

A slight smile pulled at my lips. I squinted and watched the wet, sunlit mist float through the woods. Would Lucas really come with me? I wasn't about to tell Azrael of Lucas's dislike for Neviahans and I didn't know how to tell Lucas another man would be my new lifelong fighting companion.

I tried to focus on what Azrael had said and not Korban's threats. I'm sure there would be a way for Lucas and I to be together at the sanctuary, especially if he was going to help us fight the Legion. Lucas would understand, and Azrael would behave himself. I cast a sideways glance at Azrael. Doubt washed over me when he gave me a half smile that I tried not to read into. Would Azrael behave himself?

Celestial energy constantly passed between us, making our bond stronger every moment we were in each other's presence. Every glance and every word only added to the power rushing through me. Our connection was deeper than even Starfire.

"Do you think we fought in the first Neviahan war together?" I asked, trying to understand the familiarity and comfort between us.

Azrael's questioning gaze shot to mine like I had awakened him out of his own deep thought. "Do you remember that?" he asked, his eyes wide.

I tried to remember the time before my human memories overshadowed my pre-Earth memories. The only images that came to my mind were of a misty waterfall and crystal cave. It felt like a dream from a long time ago. I shook my head. "No. Being with you just feels . . . familiar."

Azrael swallowed hard. He pressed his lips into a smile as if not allowing himself to be disappointed that I didn't remember anything from before my life on Earth. His voice was soft. "I believe we have fought many wars side by side." He captured me with those eternally deep eyes as he continued, "And there will yet be many more battles for us to fight."

I allowed myself to get lost in his eyes. "I think I would like that." I meant it sincerely. Fighting alongside him would feel like a fluid dance of grace.

"What are your earliest memories?" Azrael asked, as if still hoping to prod my pre-Earth memories.

"Well . . ." I hesitated and his curious eyes shimmered with interest. I laughed. "You really want to know?"

"Yes," Azrael said. "I want to know everything about you."

"Everything?" I asked, suddenly overwhelmed. "I don't know where to start."

"When did you first learn you were Neviahan?" Azrael asked.

That was kind of a complicated question, especially since I had denied it for so long. "My parents were killed in a fire started by a Shadow Lord," I began. "I walked away from the arson attack without even a minor burn. I think that's when I realized there was something different about me. I wasn't the only one who noticed. I was attacked by Shadow Wolves. They tried to kill me, but a witch named Hazella saved me." I watched Azrael's expression. He didn't flinch or seem surprised. "Hazella knew there was a reason why the Shadow Wolves were after me. She captured me and tortured me for information about my powers."

Azrael swallowed hard, but looked at me with eager eyes as if asking me to continue.

"I was only thirteen. I knew nothing of the Great Kingdom of Neviah, my powers, or the Shadow Legion. Although the witch was horrible, I realized that if I hadn't gone through that experience, I might not have had the courage or resiliency to accomplish all the things I have. I even discovered my powers while living with the witch."

Azrael gave me a half smile. "Most people would want revenge against such a terrible person. You could've burned her alive, but you let her go."

"I let her go a long time ago," I said. "There is too much pain in this world. Why would I want to hang on to something that has long passed?"

"How did you escape?" Azrael asked, still interested in my story.

"I met Ruburt, a dwarf from the Golden Valley. He was a goldsmith hired by the witch to make an enchanted ruby necklace. It's the same necklace I gave to Lucas to help heal him in battle."

"Enchanted?" Azrael asked.

I nodded. "Yes, I wasn't Hazella's only prisoner. The witch had also captured a pixie named Cassi and was harvesting pixie dust from her to make the necklace. When Ruburt found us, he helped us escape and led us to Oswestry. There, I was hired as a servant girl in the manor. That's where Lucas and I met. He taught me to fight. It was our dream to be knighted together." I laughed as I recalled the fond memories. "I gained favor in the sight of Lady Hannah after I used the ruby necklace to heal her. She adopted me into her house as an heir. She was wonderful to me."

"What happened to her?" Azrael asked.

I paused. After that, all my memories seemed to be coated with sadness.

"I'm sorry. If you do not want to talk about it—"

"She died." I interrupted his apology. "She died of a broken heart, and I thought my fate would be the same. We got word that two of her sons were killed on the crusade. She took off the ruby necklace that kept her alive and then she died." I could barely whisper as I told him the sad ending to Lady Hannah's life.

Azrael reached out and touched my hand as I choked back tears.

"Things got better, though." I took a deep breath, forcing myself to be strong. "I studied tactics and weaponry under some mercenaries, and as you know, I was knighted by the late king and started my mission as England's Watcher." I looked away. "I wish King Edward understood me the way his father had."

Azrael didn't ask any more questions, which was good because I had other things on my mind now. I still didn't know what to say to Edward when I got back to London. Not only had I refused to assassinate Alexander, but now I opposed King Edward's plan to forcefully unite England and Scotland.

With my mind full of doubt and terrible worries, the day quickly passed. Night came, and though the men still seemed rested, Korban insisted on stopping after Orion predicted I would fall off my horse again. I wasn't going to test his theory, so I agreed to rest for the night.

Azrael gathered firewood and stacked it neatly in a pile. I took off my gloves and held out my hands. Fire burst from my fingers and ignited the wet wood as if it were dry timber.

Azrael let out an impressed whistle.

I smiled at his compliment and sat next to the flames. Baby nuzzled against me. I hadn't realized how cold I was until the fire and the tiger's warm body started to thaw me. I shivered in the wet night air.

Orion laughed. "You'd think someone who can control fire wouldn't ever get cold."

"I don't have as much energy when the sun isn't out. I get cold easily at night." My teeth chattered as I spoke.

Korban sputtered and rolled his eyes. "Azrael complains about his energy when the weather is stale, and Orion can't get on a boat on open water."

"Yes I can," Orion objected. "I just sleep the whole time. I need to be connected with earth."

"What about you Korban?" I asked.

Korban hesitated, but then said. "My power is swordsmanship. I don't need anything except my weapons."

Azrael sat beside me and took my cold hands, warming them between his. "Neviahans need their energy source to have full strength. The sky's been overcast lately. You've been deprived of the sun's energy for some time." Azrael held my hands until I was warm again.

"Thank you." I pulled away before I burst into flames. "Aren't you worried about us being this close?"

Before Azrael could answer Orion said with a huff, "I am."

Korban nodded in agreement, and then made the sound of an explosion.

Azrael shook his head. "I'm not going to light your blood on fire." He said with reassurance. "Besides, 'tis not really your blood, but the power running through your veins that will create Starfire." His deep, calm voice penetrated me. "You must release it before I can light it, and I know you have good control over your powers."

I shook my head. "I don't have as much control as you think I do."

His eyes glimmered like a universe bursting to life. I stopped breathing. The sudden feeling of vulnerability caught me off guard. I blinked hard to stop myself from slipping into a trance. "Perhaps, we should practice before we return to London," I suggested. "Because I have no idea how to create Starfire without bleeding to death."

Azrael let out a warm laugh. "Aura, you always know how to make me smile." He put his hand over mine. "Of course we will practice. Would you like to practice now?"

"Now?" I jerked away as if I would blow up. "But I –"

"'Tis the perfect time," Azrael said. "The sun 'tis not out, which means you will be less likely to have an energy surge. You are still recovering from your injuries. 'Tis the perfect time to practice with minimal danger."

Azrael was right. Now would be a great time to practice using the power of Starfire. I mentally prepared myself by thinking about small, controlled flames instead of explosions. "Show me what I have to do." I was pleased at how brave I sounded.

Korban and Orion both slid back like I would suddenly burst into uncontrolled star flames. Even Baby slunk off into the woods.

Azrael stood and took both my hands in his to help me to my feet. "Don't do anything until I tell you," he warned in a velvet voice. Silver light glinted in his eyes, which meant he was already starting to do something with his mysterious gifts. Fire was his minor power, but I had yet to discover his major power.

He held my hands in a firm, comforting clasp, then his fingers smoldered with heat.

My heart beat fast and fierce with the excitement of discovering a new power inside me, waiting to be unleashed. Flames burst to life over our hands. I repressed the urge to add my own flames to his. I soaked his heat into my body, letting it fill me with his emotions of passion, excitement, curiosity, and hope. His comforting fire danced up my arms and down my back all the way to my feet. My hair swirled weightlessly around my face like the fire enveloping both of us. Azrael's fire rushed through my veins. My fiery blood boiled hot. I felt as if I would never be cold again.

Please remember.

His eyes were closed, his lips still. *Please remember.* I heard his voice echo again inside my head. I closed my eyes.

Can you feel this? Azrael asked without speaking.

Yes, I answered back in my mind.

This is spirit-to spirit communication. You can feel everything in my heart; see my past, present, and even my future. You can even see my dreams, desires, and fears. This is why I can never hide anything from you.

Azrael's memories played out in my mind, slow at first, then faster. I grasped onto a memory and watched Azrael fighting off the Shadow Wolves with Baby, Korban, and Orion. I even saw him lean over my body and breathe life back into me. I was relieved that I hadn't looked as bad as I had imagined.

Like flipping through the pages of a book, I saw bits of Azrael's memories. In every memory, I saw his face. I frantically examined his mask-less features before the next memory played out. When did the curse of the black mask start? I searched through his memories until I felt myself falling into a hazy darkness—the kind of darkness that surrounded me with claustrophobic suffocation. Azrael walked among the Shadow Wolves as an ally. His dark hair was spiked like daggers and his lips and eyes were lined in black as if framing the darkness of his soul.

How could this happen? Why would a Watcher, who was made to do good and help humans, fall? I remembered Azrael mentioning he had joined with the Rebellion for a short time. What if part of that evil still existed in him?

I traveled deeper into his memories, all the way to his birth and then pressed back even further. I saw something I didn't expect to see—it was me. I saw myself saying good-bye to him before he came to Earth. He ran his fingers through my hair. "I promise everything will be fine," he said. I saw myself through his eyes, and how much I was in love with him.

"I don't ever want to forget you," I said in the memory.

That memory hurt. It hurt because I did forget him. I'd forgotten everything when I was born into a human body.

I rushed through his memories until I came to the present time and saw us standing here surrounded by white energy. I pressed forward and plunged myself into his blurry future. Images of war hit me with despair. Devastation was everywhere. Frightened humans and smoldering heaps of rubble surrounded us. Events that hadn't yet happened seemed to force their way into my mind. Azrael tossed a blood ruby at the feet of a beautiful dark-haired sorceress. Molech was back, tempting Azrael to join with the Legion once again.

I pulled myself back to the presence. Scorching energy burned in my heart. I strained to repress the well of emotions and elements inside me. I felt my control slipping. My eyes sprang open, and blue flames shot from my hands into the sky. Air rushed in and out of my lungs like a whirlwind. The trees blew sideways as I exhaled.

Lightning flashed overhead. The ground rumbled at my feet. Earth essences flooded through me, mixing with the wind and fire. Energy shattered across the treetops and raced over every leaf and branch like lightning bolts.

"Keep control of the energy!" Azrael shouted above the sound of the electric wind.

I had the power of fire, wind, earth, water, life, spirit, and even death racing through me. It was like trying to wield seven long whips that sparked when they clashed together. I had to unite them and gain control. I wrangled the seven elemental streams of energy together. The elements blew out of my hands in white waves. The leaves on the trees erupted in a celestial firestorm. Starfire illuminated my skin and ran through my body like the blood in my veins.

Chaos surrounded me, then everything went still and silent as if time itself stopped.

Gentle ethereal light curved and swirled around my body like a slow whirlpool. A gown of shimmering pearl silk cloaked the contours of my body. The heavenly cloth sparkled at my slightest movement. Pink, blue, green, and gold aurora waves added to the creation pallet floating around me. I touched the energy orb surrounding me like a cocoon. It rippled in soft waves and let out a gentle soprano melody.

"The energy is moving too fast," Korban shouted. I could hear his words, but it was as if he was in a dream far away.

"She's consuming all the energy on Earth." Orion's urgent voice grew faint. "She's becoming a weapon, Azrael. You have to stop her, or she will never be able to touch another mortal again."

The sound of ocean mist brushed past my ear like a whisper. Perfect round drops of water stood suspended in the air, reflecting the light of many stars and worlds. It was the most beautiful thing I had ever seen. Nothing on Earth could compare with the divine celestial colors and lights. I reached out and touched a droplet. A delicate indigo and gold flower blossomed from the tiny element. The creation process became so clear. I immediately understood how to form life with a single touch.

I reached out and touched another sphere of water. The inhabitants of an unknown culture several galaxies away flashed through my mind. In a split second, I saw every life form on the planet and felt I knew each one individually.

Azrael sounded closer when he said, "Her energy 'tis too great. I can't reach her."

"You can, Azrael, and you must," Orion shouted. "Korban is dying."

I pulled my hand back. What had I done? I didn't know how to step out of the creation cocoon spiraling around me. "Azrael?" I whispered. My body tensed and the light whipped violently. I took in deep breaths, searching for Azrael in the tempest of energy.

A hand shot through the waves of heat and grasped mine. Azrael stepped into the cocoon. His silver eyes reflected down on me like twin mirrors. He held my glowing hand. I was shocked at how different, but beautiful my hand looked. Shimmering iridescent light wrapped around our bodies.

"'Tis your true form. What you look like without your human body," Azrael answered.

"Did I destroy my human body?" I asked.

Azrael shook his head. "No, but you need to come back now or you will not be able to stay here on Earth anymore. We need you, and the longer you are in this form, the more your mortal body dies."

Chapter Ten

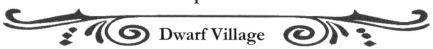 Dwarf Village

We should let her sleep," Azrael said.

"We have to keep movin'," whispered Orion.

"Mortals need to sleep, and she's had little the last week," Azrael explained.

"After what happened last night, she might sleep for another week. Just think of what damage she could've done if she were one of the Immortals."

I tried to make sense of what they said before remembering the Starfire experience. What had I done? My eyes sprang open and I lunged forward.

Orion jumped back, his eyes wide with surprise. I probably looked just as startled as he did before he let out a bellowing laugh.

"Aura." Azrael leaned forward and grasped my shoulder with a firm but gentle grip. "Are you all right?"

I didn't answer his question because I didn't know if I was all right or not. "Where are we?" I sat up and brushed back my tangled hair. "What time is it?" The sun shone through the leafy trees overhead, but I couldn't tell its position in the sky. They must have moved me to a different location because there was no evidence of the damage I had caused. I could have killed someone. My heart dropped. What if I had killed someone? I whirled around. "Where are Korban and Baby?"

"Baby 'tis hunting, and Korban . . ." Azrael nodded his head toward a bright patch of sunlight. Korban's body lay strewn out in the sun. I watched his chest to see if he breathed. His body lay completely motionless.

I covered my mouth to muffle my horrified gasp. "Is he . . ." I stopped myself. He couldn't be dead.

"He'll be fine," Orion assured me. "That lazy bum is in survival sleep."

"Survival sleep?" I asked, blinking away tears of guilt.

Azrael threw Orion a warning glare.

Orion cleared his throat and amended, "His body, 'tis healin'."

"Healing?" I whispered so my voice wouldn't crack with emotion.

Orion laughed. "He got too close and you knocked him out cold."

"Oh, no!" I dropped my head in my hands. Starfire was too powerful for me to control. I really didn't mean to hurt anyone. "I could have killed all of you."

Orion crossed his arms. "You probably would 'ave if ye'd been at full strength."

"We have bigger problems to worry about," Azrael said. "We crossed into England's borders last night. The Shadow Legion patrols this area, so we need to find a safe place to rest until Korban awakes."

There had to be somewhere we could go. Someplace with friends we could trust. I sat up taller and leaned forward. "I know a town where we can stay. The people there are allies to Watchers."

"Where is this place?" Azrael asked suspiciously.

I brightened my tone. "It's in the Golden Valley."

"Aye, is that where the dwarves live?" Orion asked.

I nodded. "Yes, perhaps Ruburt still lives there."

Azrael stroked his unshaven face. "The Golden Valley 'tis close. We can be there by nightfall."

"I say we go," Orion agreed.

A massive force slammed against my back in an affectionate nuzzle. I caught my balance and turned to see Baby. "There you are." I wrapped my arms around his fluffy neck. The colossal kitty laid his head on my lap, pinning me to the ground. I ran my fingers through his silky fur.

Azrael pulled my hand from Baby's coat and held it to get my attention. "Do you need to sleep?" He sounded overly concerned.

"That wasn't a small light show you put on last night. I don't want you pushing yourself."

I looked down at his hand holding mine and remembered the way his soul was exposed to me. Part of him would always be inside me now. I pulled away and shook my head. "I'm fine."

Orion scooped Korban up and tossed his motionless body over his horse. "We are down one fighter. We can't afford to lose you too, Aura."

I pursed my lips. "I'm not going to fall off my horse, Orion," I assured.

A deafening roar cut through the forest. My heart jumped and I whirled around. The sun dimmed and the air chilled my skin like a sudden frost. Smoky clouds rolled across the sky from the east. They weren't like any clouds I had ever seen before. I watched the fast-moving shroud devour all light in its path.

"What is that?" I asked as the black storm moved across the sky toward us.

Orion swung his leg over his horse and cursed.

Azrael took my hand and pulled me to my horse. "It looks like we have less time than we thought," he murmured. "The Rebellion 'tis veiling the sun. It makes us weaker while given them an advantage in the darkness. They are preparing for war."

"Erebus?" The Shadow King's name came out in a gasp. I bent down and lifted my horse's saddle. It felt heavier than usual after my Starfire explosion.

Azrael snatched my saddle with one hand, tossed it onto my horse, and buckled the straps with ease. I tried not to look impressed by his display of strength. Like Samson, maybe Azrael's power was inhuman strength.

"Stay on your guard," Azrael warned. "Not only do we have the Shadow Legion to worry about, but thieves and assassins patrol these woods."

I swung my leg over my horse and turned south. I wasn't too worried about thieves or assassins. Even though our caravan was small, Azrael's huge tiger was sure to scare off anyone who might think about ambushing us.

We didn't talk much as we urged our horses into a gallop. Guilt over hurting Korban ate at me, and worry for Lucas consumed me with anguish. I had put people I cared about in danger. What if Lucas was dead? And Korban . . . I looked at Korban's limp body bouncing over the saddle as we rode. He looked dead. Orion and Azrael didn't seem worried and planned to tease him when he awoke. Starfire was too dangerous. I couldn't control it. There had to be another way to defeat Erebus.

Azrael glanced over his shoulder. We made eye contact and then he looked away. Last night, when he awoke Starfire within me, glimpses of his dreams, dark secrets, sins, and desires, along with a few of his memories meshed with mine. I even saw a vague future, full of war.

This wasn't good. Our bond was already too strong. I was worried I might be falling in love with him, but I had to stay true to Lucas who had stayed loyal to me. I let out a frustrated sigh. Only the most horrible woman in the world would dump a longtime friend for someone she just met . . . or at least, just met on Earth. I remembered Azrael's memory of us from before Earth life. Was our commitment to each other deeper and stronger than any other?

There were a few things I wanted to talk with him about aside from his Watcher powers. I couldn't help but be terrified by his dark past with the Shadow Legion. What had he done as the servant of Erebus? What if he had killed humans or even other Neviahans? What if someday he turned back to the dark armies and abandoned us? His future sent waves of doubt through my mind.

Azrael whirled around and pinched his eyebrows together in concern.

I took a breath and I smiled like everything was all right until he looked away. "Focus, Auriella," I told myself. I had a bad habit of asking ridiculous "what if" questions until I got worked up. I had to stay grounded and concentrate on what I needed to do. Too many people depended on me. I shook my head. There would be time to figure out the problem with Lucas and Azrael after I destroyed Erebus.

We rode hard, outracing the dark storm. It wasn't long before we reached the Golden Valley. I could only imagine what the dwarves thought when we rode down the main street of their village. Korban looked like a dead man draped over Orion's horse and our clothes were singed from the Starfire incident. Then there was Baby. We must have looked like a freak show, or invaders. The dwarves seemed unsure as to whether they should run and hide or stay and watch.

With the storm behind us the setting sun glowed red over the western hills. If Ruburt wasn't here, no one would take us in and we would have to spend another night in the cold rebel-infested woods.

A wooden sign swung on sterling hinges over a smithy shop. I read the words out loud, "Ruburt's Metal Works." I clasped my hands and turned to Azrael and Orion. "This has to be it." I dismounted and tapped on the door. From inside, metal stopped clanking and footsteps grew louder. "We're closed," grouched a deep, familiar voice.

"Ruburt," I said through the door. "It's me, Auriella."

The door cracked open. Ruburt's gaze lifted until he met my eyes. "Lady Auriella!" His smile and stocky frame was exactly the way I remembered. His sparkling brown eyes complimented his dark hair. He still tied his long beard in a knot to keep from stepping on it. A few streaks of gray lined his somewhat balding head, and a few more age spots dotted his strong, calloused hands. He swung the door open wide. "Come in." He gestured inside the massive metal shop. "These are your friends?"

I nodded. "Yes."

"It looks like one of 'em isn't doin' so good."

Azrael took Korban off the horse.

"I accidentally knocked him out last night," I admitted.

Ruburt let out a hearty laugh. "You haven't changed a bit, Auriella."

We followed Ruburt into the shop. He stepped back and his jaw tightened when Baby wedged himself through the door.

The oven glowed with heat while the last of the sunlight streaked through the windows. Hammers, tongs, etching tools, and metal files lay scattered over the tabletops. A bucket of bent nails sat next to the fire. A plow, sickles, and other farming tools lined the walls. Ruburt worked too hard and still overwhelmed himself with projects.

Ruburt shut the door and locked it, then drew the curtains over the windows. The room went dark except for the orange glow pulsing from the oven. "Does the Rebellion know you are here?" he asked in hushed tones.

"No," I assured. "But we are being tracked. We saw Erebus's dark fog covering the forest to the east."

Ruburt lit an oil lamp and moved a few things off his tables so Azrael could lay Korban down.

"Looks like he's dead," Ruburt mumbled.

"He's in survival sleep." Orion shrugged his shoulders as if such abilities were common knowledge.

Ruburt stroked his long beard. "Then he could be asleep for a while." He turned to me. "You came to the right place. My people will be more than happy to host the Lady of Neviah and her friends."

"Hopefully not for too long," I added. "We don't want to put your village in any danger, but we didn't know where else to go." I motioned toward my traveling companions, and then realized I hadn't introduced them yet. "Forgive me. Ruburt, meet Orion and Azrael."

Ruburt shook their hands. "Both Neviahan Watchers, I presume?" They nodded. "Why don't you come to my cottage tonight for dinner?" Ruburt offered. "I'm sure Pearl would love to meet you."

"Pearl?" I asked, not recognizing the name.

"My wife." Ruburt beamed and blushed.

I clasped my hands together. "Oh, Ruburt! I'm so happy for you."

When we first met, he had sworn never to get involved with women. I was glad he changed his mind—he deserved all the happiness in the world.

Azrael put his hand on my shoulder. "You should go to dinner. Orion and I are going to scout the woods for rebel spies." Azrael motioned toward Korban and asked Ruburt, "May we leave him here?"

"Of course," Ruburt said. "He doesn't look like he's goin' anywhere."

Azrael, Orion, and Baby left the smithy shop to secure the surrounding woods. I walked with Ruburt down a dusty road toward his cottage.

"What are you goin' to do now?" he asked.

I shook my head. "I'm not sure. I feel like an outcast in my own country. Can you believe the king sent me on an assassination mission? Edward ordered me to leave the castle and kill a human for his own personal gain."

"Did you warn the king 'bout the Shadow Legion and their plans?" Ruburt asked.

"I warned him a hundred times." I dropped my hands to my sides.

"Did King Edward place armies under your command?" Ruburt prodded.

"Ruburt," I said half-heartedly, "why would the king give me armies? I'm a woman. The king has issues with women in leadership positions—especially military leadership positions."

The lamp swung from Ruburt's hand, lighting the road just ahead of us. "You are the only one who could protect London. Watchers stay in the city they are to protect, unless they are dismissed by the Neviahan druids, or . . ." He stopped and held one finger in the air as if making an important point. "Or if the humans no longer have faith in them as Watchers. That's when the Watcher must move on."

I gasped. "No." It couldn't be true.

"Your responsibility isn't in London anymore," Ruburt said frankly.

I pulled my hair over my shoulder and wrung it in my fists. "What am I going to do?" If I wasn't the Watcher of London any more, where did I belong? I thought about my promise to return to the sanctuary with Azrael. At this point, it seemed like the best solution for me, but I still didn't want to leave London.

"Sometimes you act so human," Ruburt sputtered with amazement.

"What does that mean?" I tried not to laugh at his too-serious tone.

"As much as you love London, it's not your home. Earth isn't even your home. Earth is your battleground. You've never been to the Neviahan sanctuary. You've never been trained properly. You don't even know who you are."

"I'm the Lady of Neviah," I said to counter his statement.

Ruburt raised one eyebrow. "Do you know what that means?" I was glad he didn't wait for an answer, because I had no answer. "You have to leave the human world."

I stopped breathing as my thoughts realigned. I couldn't get too attached to any one place or any Earthy possession. I had to keep fighting. I had to stay on guard. I had to help my people win this war against Erebus and the Shadow Legion.

Ruburt continued, "One day you will go back to Neviah. Not everyone is as lucky as the few Neviahan Immortals who will fight on Earth until Erebus is defeated."

My interest was piqued. I had heard of them, but didn't know much about the Immortals. Before my parents died, they told me bedtime stories about the Lady of Neviah and the Immortals. My heart ached to remember the details of the story. "How do you know all this, Ruburt?" I asked.

Ruburt chuckled. "It's part of the legends." Lamp lights glittered from a small cottage in a meadow just ahead of us. "Would you like to hear more 'bout it?"

"Of course," I said.

"Come inside and I will tell you all 'bout it," Ruburt said.

I ducked and followed Ruburt through the doorway of his miniature house.

"Ruburt, is that you?" called a sweet voice from the kitchen.

"Yes, Pearl, I'm home," Ruburt answered.

"Workin' late again, I presume." A darling middle-aged dwarf woman stepped around the corner and dropped the rag she carried. "Mercy me." Pearl placed her hand over her heart.

"This is Pearl, my wife," Ruburt said. I curtsied and Ruburt continued, "And this is Auriella, the Lady of Neviah."

"I never thought I would see the Lady of Neviah with my own eyes, let alone have her in my home." Pearl glanced around the cottage and obsessively started tidying the room.

A young dwarf girl with dark hair entered, carrying a cornhusk doll.

"This is our daughter, Kassi," Ruburt said.

"Kassi. Like our pixie friend, Cassi," Auriella asked.

Ruburt mumbled something, then said out loud. "That jealous pixie left after Pearl and I got married. Cassi is probably in the woods causing mischief for someone else now."

"Why are you dressed funny?" Kassi asked, looking at my burnt clothes.

Pearl covered her daughter's mouth. "That's not polite."

"It's all right," I said. "I'm dressed like this because I was practicing for a fight."

"A fight?" Kassi's eyes went wide.

I didn't want the young girl to be frightened by the thought of monsters, so I quickly added, "There are many warriors looking out for you, so there is no need for nightmares tonight."

"Yes," Pearl said. "And it's past your bedtime."

"Please tell me a story?" Kassi begged.

Ruburt scooped his daughter into his arms and sat in a cushioned rocking chair. "It's my turn to tell the bedtime story tonight," he said.

I had a feeling this was the story Ruburt promised to tell me about the Immortals. Like a child, I sat on the rug at Ruburt's feet.

"Once upon a time," Ruburt started majestically, "in a magical kingdom far, far away, there was a mighty king. This king was so powerful he could control stars and worlds without number."

"Whoa!" Kassi's eyes glittered with excitement.

Ruburt continued, "The Great King had seven sons who were the high princes of the land. Each of 'em had enormous power, but they used their powers for different purposes. The eldest son had the power of life. He could connect with and have empathy for all living things."

"Em-pa-thi?" Kassi sounded out. "What's that?"

"It means he could feel what others felt and experience what they were going through. He could also hear your thoughts, and see your past and future. The moment the high prince met you, he knew everything about you."

I could only imagine how exhausting a power like that would be. I had a portion of Azrael's thoughts and memories, and it was more than enough for me to deal with.

Ruburt made eye contact with me, and then went back to his story. "Everyone in the kingdom agreed that besides the king himself, the first high prince was the most powerful man in all the twelve Neviahan galaxies—everyone agreed except the second prince." Ruburt's voice deepened with suspense. "The second prince thought he was the most powerful man in the universe, even more powerful than the king himself. Do you know his name?"

Kassi leaned forward and whispered, "Erebus."

My heart jumped inside my chest at the mention of the dark prince's name.

"When the king rewarded the first prince dominion over the twelve galaxies, Erebus became enraged. Erebus controlled the elemental gift of death. Death destroys life and he thought he could destroy the first high prince. He set out to prove he was the most powerful."

"What did he do, Daddy?" Kassi asked.

"Since Erebus couldn't kill anyone while in the Kingdom of Neviah he convinced one-third of the kingdom to rebel. He thought he could overthrow the king and the first high prince. Many Neviahans resisted, including Lady Auriella."

Kassi turned and beamed at me with admiration. I smiled back, though I didn't feel I deserved the approbation. After all, I didn't remember any of this.

"The kingdom divided into two groups: the Rebels and the Resisters. Then came the first great Neviahan war. It wasn't a war with weapons, but a war of Neviahan power. We don't know how long they fought, but the Resisters eventually won and drove the Rebellion out of the Great Kingdom of Neviah!" Ruburt said triumphantly.

Kassi cheered.

I smiled and desperately wished I could remember that victorious battle.

Ruburt leaned forward, his voice full of intensity. "But the war wasn't over yet." He paused dramatically. "Erebus was arrogant enough to think he could create a new kingdom for himself and his followers. That's when the rebels came to Earth."

Kassi snuggled into Ruburt's chest and he brushed back her hair. "Don't be scared, Kassi. The King of Neviah sent good warriors to Earth to protect us. They're our Watchers." Ruburt looked up and met my eyes. "The Watchers are going to save Earth and destroy all the rebels."

"Lady Auriella is going to protect us?" Kassi asked.

"Yes," I answered resolutely. "I am." I didn't know how I was going to do it, but I would defeat Erebus.

"Lady Auriella won't be alone," Ruburt added. "There are thousands of Neviahans, and millions more who will be born onto this planet. Some of them are even granted immortality by the Great King of Neviah. Their human body is changed in the blink of an eye. These warriors are almost indestructible, and will stay on Earth until Erebus is destroyed. They are the ones the Rebellion fear the most." Ruburt emphasized each of his next words, "And Lady Auriella is going to lead the Immortals in battle."

Chapter Eleven

Starlight Pond

I awoke in Ruburt's barn loft. Pearl felt awful for not having more suitable accommodations for me, but I assured her that the loft was more than luxurious. Pearl had cleaned the loft, laid down fresh hay for a bed, and provided me with several of her best quilts.

I brushed my hair back and blinked the sleep from my eyes. The midday sunlight streamed through the cracks in the walls and shattered off my skin. My Lifelight glittered with iridescent colors.

I had stayed up too late wondering about my mission. I couldn't get Ruburt's story off my mind. How was I supposed to lead an army of immortal warriors? After the accident with Starfire, I felt inadequate as a warrior, let alone one who was expected to lead such a powerful group of beings.

I sat up and smacked my head against the ceiling. "Ow!" I squinted and put my hand over my head. "Brilliant!" I rolled my eyes at my clumsiness. The miniature dwarf village would take some getting used to.

I bounded from the loft in one jump, and felt like a giant walking through the stables past Ruburt's butterscotch pony.

In the meadow surrounding Ruburt's cottage, the sounds of swishing tails and the soft tearing of grass accompanied my midnight black horse, along with the other horses as they grazed.

I made my way to the cottage and knocked on the door. Pearl's eyes lit up when she saw me. "Lady Auriella. I'm just about finished pressing your new dress."

"New dress? Oh, Pearl." I sat down. "You didn't have to—."

"Oh yes I did. I'll not be 'aving the Lady of Neviah wearing. . ." She paused as if trying to figure out what I was wearing.

"Thank you," I said to break the awkward silence. "It will be nice having something less tattered and charred to wear." I stared at the dress. It was green—Azrael's favorite color. There were so many things I knew about Azrael now—things he had never told me. Azrael's memories replayed in my mind. I couldn't get him out of my head and that frightened me.

"What's troublin' you, Lady Auriella?" Pearl sat beside me. I let out a long sigh and shook my head. Did she really want to hear about my absurd worries? She smiled at me. "I may not have the powers of a Watcher, but I'm still a woman and can sense when something's wrong."

I gave her a soft smile. "My problem is complicated. I'm not sure how to explain it."

Pearl gave my hand a reassuring pat. "Try."

I crumpled. I couldn't hold this in. I needed someone to talk to, and not just anyone. Pearl was another woman who wouldn't judge me, who didn't care about politics and who understood my position as a Neviahan. I took in a deep breath and began, "I was engaged to a man several years ago. I got word he was killed in battle and moved on with my life. Then he returned, but things weren't the same.

"When I met Azrael, I felt this connection I've never felt with anyone before." I let out a long sigh. "When our hands touched, sparks literally flew from our fingertips as if drawing us together. I have no doubt that we knew each other in Neviah." I shook my head and glanced at Pearl. Her face was filled with kindness and compassion. I continued, "The situation got complicated because I'm still engaged to Lucas." I tried to blink away the melancholy haze from my eyes. "It's still hard to believe this isn't just another dream. I swear I'll wake up and he'll be gone again." I stopped and looked away. "Even if I marry Lucas, I will have to see Azrael, feel his soul, and combine my powers with his. It's an intimate connection that I can never have with Lucas. Is what I'm feeling for Azrael more than just Starfire?"

I looked to Pearl and welcomed any advice.

"Do you love Lucas?" she asked.

I answered with a nod.

"Do you love Azrael?"

I broke my regal composure and wrapped my arms around my stomach. "I don't know." I pressed my hands against my face. "I don't know if I'm in love with him. I don't know if I'm in love with either of them."

Pearl took my hands in hers. "Sometimes the hardest decisions are when we have to choose between two good things. If Lucas loves you as much as you say he does, he will hold off the engagement until you know for sure. Don't try to complicate this more than it already is. Open your heart and the man you are destined to be with will naturally fill that void."

I paused, frozen with fear at the thought of opening my heart and letting someone in. It was easy and safe to go through the motions, doing what everyone expected me to do.

"You're awake," Ruburt's voice came from behind us.

I spun around and forced a cheery smile on my face. "Good morning, Ruburt."

"It's almost evenin'," he mumbled. "The boys are debatin' if you're in survival sleep."

I laughed. "Tell them yes. I desperately needed that sleep." I leaned forward and said in a more serious tone, "How is Korban?"

Ruburt shook his head. "Still unconscious. You won't be travelin' with him in that condition."

I lowered my head. As long as we stayed in the Golden Valley, all the dwarves were in danger. The Shadow Legion didn't give up easily. Even a small pack of Shadow Wolves could destroy the tiny village.

Pearl put the freshly pressed dress in my arms. "You've slept through breakfast and lunch. I expect you to make up for it. I've fixed oatmeal, honey wheat bread, scones, and rabbit stew."

I looked into the kitchen. Loaves of bread garnished the table, along with several pots. Why did Pearl make so much? "Did Orion and Azrael eat?" I asked.

Pearl shook her head. "No."

I raised one eyebrow. "What time did they return to the shop?"

"Not until this morning," Ruburt answered.

"I suppose they already ate," Pearl mused. "Azrael was the one who brought us the rabbits. He seemed quite adamant you get a good meal."

I knelt next to the miniature kitchen table. Pearl brought the dishes to the table until the meal covered the whole surface. "I hope you have a healthy appetite because we won't have ice until winter comes. Food doesn't keep on its own, you know."

I ate as much as I could, but there was no way I could eat all Pearl had prepared.

Pearl shook her head as if she was disappointed in me. "You better go get cleaned up before the daylight is spent. There's a pond on the edge of the forest about a half a mile from here. Just follow the trail."

I picked up the new dress and held it against my chest. "Thank you, Pearl. I'm sure once I'm clean, I will feel human again."

Ruburt cleared his throat.

"I meant, I will feel like a Neviahan again." I paused in the doorway and turned to Pearl. "Thank you for the advice."

Pearl's rosy cheeks lifted when she smiled.

I left and followed a narrow trail toward a cluster of trees surrounding the pond. The sun dipped below the tree line and the horizon glowed with gold and orange light. Once in the privacy of the grove, I peeled the tattered clothing from my body and assessed the damage. The sleeves were burnt to the elbows, my skirt irreparable.

I dangled one foot in the cold water. I thought about using my powers to warm the water, but the pond was full of fish that Ruburt's family used for food. I pressed away from the bank and immersed myself. My tense muscles relaxed as my battle-beaten, travel-worn body adjusted to the temperature.

The thought of loving two men terrified me, but Pearl was right. I needed to open my heart and allow the void to be filled naturally. Everything would work out in the end.

I waded back to the bank for the soap and lathered my body. Soot, ash, and dirt floated from my skin across the water. I must have looked completely war ravaged. I rinsed the last bit of soap from my body and let the gravel on the bottom of the pond massage my feet as I soaked in the water.

The sun set and the first few stars appeared overhead. I pulled myself out of the water, dried, and slipped the fresh cloth next to my skin.

For the first time since I left London, I felt renewed. Instead of using the heat of my powers to dry my hair, I let the long red waves hold the moisture and stick to the exposed skin on my back. I took a deep breath and held the feeling of newness near me a moment longer.

Reaching into the pond, I took a pebble from the water. My warm fingers curled around the rock and stole the cool radiance of the stone. As soon as Korban awoke, we would return to London and fight Erebus and his army. After that, I didn't know what would happen. Everything in my life felt like chaos and I wanted to do the right thing. I just didn't know what the right thing was.

I dropped the pebble into the water and let it shatter my reflection. The waves rippled, then stood as still as glass, mirroring the brilliant silvery moon and sprinkled stars across the heavens. A strong breeze broke the flawless water. The wind caught the edge of my dress and tousled it with the long grass. I wrapped my arms around myself as a feeble shield against the cold night air. I took in a deep breath of the wind and let it fill me with a moment of peace.

Across the pond, a pair of eyes glowed between the dark trees. My heart sprinted as the creature stared at me. I held my breath and took a step back. They found me. The Shadow Wolves always traveled in packs—where there was one, there were always more. A hand touched my shoulder from behind. I let out a sharp shriek and whirled around ready to fight.

"Shhh. 'Tis just me." Azrael grinned, obviously amused by my startled reaction. His eyes shimmered behind his dark mask.

I cupped my hand over his mouth, hushing him. "There's something on the other side of the water," I whispered. "Shadow Wolf."

Azrael looked up sharply and eyed the woods. He unfastened his cloak and wrapped it around my shoulders. It still held the warmth of his body and intoxicating scent of leather and spruce. "Stay here. I'll investigate."

Azrael snuck around the pond near the pair of glowing eyes. A creature the size of a bear reared up and roared. "Auriella, stay where you are. 'Tis a ferocious beast. I can handle this."

"I'm coming to help you!" I picked up a few stones and a long stick. Men were so stubborn and never asked for help.

"No, no. I've got it," he assured me.

In the darkness, I couldn't make out the details of the beast. The creature charged at Azrael and knocked him to the ground. "Ah, gentle," he said in hushed tones. Something strange was going on.

The beast roared again, then went silent. Azrael stood and bounded toward me like a boyish warrior who just won a game. He grinned and held his chest high.

"Are you all right?" I frantically ran my hands up his arms to make sure he wasn't damaged. "Are you hurt?"

He took note of my hands and his smile grew wider. "'Twas a forest beast."

"A forest beast?" I gasped.

He nodded. "Yes, very dangerous."

"What a ridiculous thing for you to do. You weren't even armed. Let me see if you are hurt." I examined him in the moonlight. Not even a scratch. I felt his solid chest, his heavy breath and quickening heartbeat. What kind of a half-wit runs into the woods and wrestles a forest beast with his bare hands? "Do you want to be in survival sleep like Korban?" I scolded.

From the corner of my eye, I saw Baby's silhouette stalking off into the woods. It was a trick. Azrael was only trying to impress me.

"Azrael, why are you doing this?" I turned and focused on the stars overhead. "Don't you know I'm already impressed with you? You don't need to prove anything to me. I've already felt your soul. I know your intentions and all your dreams." I took a deep breath and whispered, "You haunt me." A moment of silence passed. I waited for him to leave, but he didn't.

He reached for my hand, but pulled away in a repentant manner. "Auriella," he started, "Since we are speaking so openly, please tell me what I can do to win your heart and hand in marriage."

I dropped my shoulders. "Azrael, you don't need to try. I'm afraid my heart already belongs to you, but my hand belongs to someone else." I turned toward the cottage and walked away from him. I couldn't talk about this anymore. It was too painful.

Azrael caught up and took my hand. White sparks flew from his fingertips and skittered up my forearm. "When I first saw you, I stopped breathing. I still feel like I'm holding my breath." Azrael lifted my hand to his lips. "But if all I ever get on Earth is your heart, I will be more than satisfied."

I leaned into him and held my hand against his chest. His heart beat fiercely under my touch. He wrapped his arms around me in a secure embrace that felt like a natural mold for my body. Energy flew from the woods and danced around us. I did love him and I realized this wasn't just a reaction or side effect of Starfire. I desperately wanted to yank the mask off his face and see him for the first time. Everything about him was familiar and comforting.

Azrael brushed back my hair. "When we used Starfire, you saw all my desires. Please tell me what you desire."

"You know what I want," I said. "I just want to do the right thing."

His gaze captured mine and smoldered with passion. He leaned forward, pressing closer. His hand curled around my waist to the small of my back and drew me in.

The more we touched, the more I struggled to keep the tsunami of energy from bursting out of me. The power of Starfire was too dangerous for us to be together like this.

I held my hand between us to stop his welcomed, but forbidden advance. My fingertips trickled with white smoke as the fire he ignited rushed through my veins like hot adrenaline. I clenched my hands into fists and lowered my head in retreat. "And you know why we can't do this."

Azrael must have realized what was happening because he took a step back and blinked away the fire in his eyes. "Not yet, at least," he whispered. He squared his shoulders and stood like a disciplined military soldier. "Know this." His voice grew intense. "I want the same thing you do." His fingers wove between mine and seized my hand in an embrace. My hand burst to flames in his grip. I tried to jerk away before we caused another Starfire explosion.

He clutched tighter, letting the flames grow in a scorching dance around our interlocked hands. "Someday we will find a way to be together," he promised and pulled away before our fire got out of control.

I wrangled my emotions and smothered the flames. My touch was a weapon to which only he was immune, but it was no excuse for losing control of my feelings.

His lips turned up in a velvet smile. "You don't always say what you're feeling." He looked at his hand, still perfect and unmarked by the fire bath. "At least this way I can feel what you are feeling."

Chapter Twelve

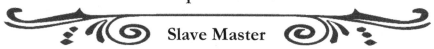

Slave Master

The sun shone through the tailor shop window and beamed across the bright threads. I wove a wooden needle through a loom and pressed the threads down with a comb. Kassi played with ragdolls in the back of Pearl's seamstress shop and broke up the menial silence of our work with playful giggles. Pearl measured another piece of cloth and pinned it in several places. She noticed me watching her and asked, "Any word on Korban?"

I dropped my shoulders "No, and it's been almost a week." I wove another thread through the loom. "As much as I love being with you and Ruburt, the longer we stay here, the longer your village is in danger."

Pearl flipped her hand through the air. "The Shadow Legion has never crossed our borders."

I still worried. Every night, the armies of darkness hunted for us. It was only a matter of time before the Blood Hunters would pick up our scent. We couldn't stay here much longer—I had to get back to

London. I debated whether I should go on my own and leave Azrael and Orion with Korban until he awoke. I shook my head. Azrael would never agree to that idea. If I tried to sneak away, I knew he could out-ride me, and I wasn't going to push my horse after the recent wolf attack. There had to be something I could do. I hated just waiting for the wolves to find us.

A shrill scream from outside the shop startled me from my thoughts.

"What in the world could that be?" Pearl asked.

I jumped up from the loom and raced to the window.

Two large men flung a dwarf into the back of a wagon. Half a dozen men chased after dwarven women and children. Several other dwarves fought to get out of the wagon.

My jaw tightened as I clenched my teeth together. I turned to Pearl and instructed, "Take Kassi and run home. Stay hidden until Ruburt or I come for you."

I burst from the shop and instinctively reached to draw my sword as Pearl and Kassi ran down the road toward their cottage. My fingers grasped air and I rolled my eyes at my own folly. I couldn't believe I was caught unarmed again. I had asked Ruburt to sharpen my sword for me last night.

At least I wasn't alone. Azrael and Orion argued with a man who appeared to be the leader. Orion crossed his arms, making his muscles bulge. Azrael kept one hand on the hilt of his sword.

Ruburt raced to me, his eyes wide with horror. "Pearl and Kassi—are they. . ."

"They're safe. I told them to go home," I said.

Ruburt let out a deep sigh of relief and fought to catch his breath. "These are the same slave merchants who came last year and took some of our people."

I narrowed my eyes as rage sweltered inside me. "They're not taking anyone this time." I sprinted across the muddy road toward the wagon, ready to assist Azrael and Orion in battle against the slave merchants if necessary.

"Release the dwarves," Azrael bellowed. "This town 'tis a sanctuary and you're not welcome here." If I hadn't been angry myself, I would've been startled to hear Azrael's gentle voice sound so fierce.

"You can't stop us." The slave master's lip curled into a devilish smile. "With two men? Even my weakest warrior can crush you." Of course I was offended that he didn't acknowledge me.

Azrael put his hands on his hips and leaned back. "Oh, really? Should we have a duel, then? If our best warrior wins, you leave and never come back. If your best warrior wins, we will purchase every slave in the wagon from you."

The slave master eyed the wagon full of dwarves and nodded. "Agreed."

Azrael spun around and whispered in a confident tone, "They have no idea what a foolish bet they have made."

I smirked. Orion or Azrael could easily defeat the slave master's best warrior. I could already see the epic victory in my mind. Azrael unsheathed his sword and handed it to me. "Try not to be too rough on him. If he dies, we will have to fight all of them."

I met his eyes and tried to read the intentions behind his dark mask. Was he really suggesting that I was the best warrior of the three of us?

The slave master erupted in laughter. "Her? Now this will be entertaining. I would like to see this wisp of a lass fight my champion."

I gripped the hilt of the sword and stepped forward. It felt good to have a blade in my hands again. If I couldn't fight the Rebellion in London, I was more than happy to fight injustice elsewhere.

"You agreed to fight our best warrior." Azrael motioned toward me. I squared my shoulders and stood ready.

"This is the best you've got?" The slave master roared with laughter. I knew how I must look to him. I was in one of my lovely dresses and gripping Azrael's Celtic broad-sword.

My challenger stepped forward. He stood almost as tall as Orion, and veins lined his muscular arms. He spat on the ground and grinned wickedly at me, showing his tobacco-stained teeth. It didn't matter how big or strong he looked—I knew he was a coward. Only a coward would abduct innocent women and children.

My hands smoldered with heat. I took a deep breath to control the angry fire raging inside me. As much as I wanted to, I couldn't use my powers in this battle. The slave merchants would know we were Neviahan and report us to the Legion.

The warrior cracked his knuckles and gripped his sword. The sun glistened off his bald head and the gold hoop ring that dangled from his ear. He tossed off his shirt to reveal a muscular chest covered in scars and sloppy tattoos.

I was not amused. I elegantly lifted my gown from the muddy road with my free hand. I wasn't about to let one of my best dresses get dirty.

The thug bellowed a war cry and charged toward me. He swung his blade with all his strength, but over-extended. I wove the tip of my sword into his hand guard and flung it into the air and onto the mud. I couldn't believe the novice mistake he made.

The dwarves cheered from the side of the road.

"Slave master," I taunted, still holding my skirt like a lady. "How am I supposed to fight your champion if he does not have his weapon?" I tilted my head and gave him an overly innocent smile. I intentionally moved with more feminine elegance to insult him.

The dwarves laughed. The slave master grunted.

Hot blood sped through my veins. Adrenalin quickened my senses. I kicked my challenger's muddy sword back to him. "I see this is not fair. I will fight two of your men."

The slave master shouted, ordering another man to attack me.

Azrael and Orion laughed at the brutes struggling to keep up with me. One charged toward me. I stepped out of the way at the last moment. The slave merchant's momentum propelled him forward as he slid in the mud. Another round of laughter came from the gathering crowd of dwarves. I had to admit I was having fun. The large tattooed slave merchant swung his sword at me like a club. I couldn't believe he made the same novice mistake twice. I disarmed him again. I released the hand on my dress and picked up the fallen sword. The other fighter scrambling to his feet, ready to attack afresh. I locked his sword between the two blades I now held. I kicked, hurling him back into the mud, and then held up all three swords. "It seems this is still not a fair fight, two men against a maiden. Send me a third man!" I called to the slave master.

The slave master reluctantly motioned to the wagon and several men unlocked the door. Azrael and Orion helped the dwarves from the wagon.

I needed this. I needed to feel like someone's hero again. Serving others was the cure for my self-pity and feelings of helplessness. I returned to Azrael and held out the hilt of his weapon to him. "Thank you for having faith in me."

Azrael's eyes sparkled in that majestic way I would never get used to. "There never was a doubt in my mind," he said. "You are the strongest warrior I've ever met." He put his hand on the hilt of his sword and pushed it toward me. "Keep it."

"Your sword?" This wasn't like a bouquet of flowers or even a new dress. This was his weapon. "No, I can't take it."

Azrael put his hand over mine. "'Tis yours now. In our culture, once you win a battle with a weapon, it becomes yours." He turned back to the wagon as a silent way of saying that the conversation was over.

I couldn't help but feel tricked into receiving a valuable gift from him.

Ruburt raced toward me with a huge grin on his face. "You fight like a she-bear defending her cubs. You're undoubtedly the most terrifying woman they've ever seen." He chuckled in his deep, comforting voice. "The slave master was right about one thing—that was entertaining."

"Pearl and Kassi," I remembered out loud. "We need to let them know we're safe."

Ruburt and I started for the cottage in the meadow. I looked back and met the slave master's gaze. His eyes flashed with revenge. His face flared red and the veins in his neck pulsed. He snatched a dagger from his belt and charged toward Azrael.

"No! Azrael, look out!" I screamed.

Azrael whirled around. The slave master plunged the blade toward Azrael, slashing the dagger across his chest. Gold sparks sprayed off Azrael's body like iron hitting perfect steel. Azrael reached out with inhuman speed, snatched the sharp edge of the blade in his bare hand, and crushed the metal.

"What the devil?" The slave master said.

"Demons!" The slave merchants scattered in confusion.

I covered my mouth to keep from screaming. The event replayed in my mind as I tried to make sense of what had just happened.

"I knew it," Ruburt mumbled. "I knew they were Immortals."

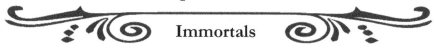 Immortals

I raised my eyebrow. "Immortal?"

Azrael's hand shot to my lips, hushing me. He snatched my wrist and pulled me inside Ruburt's shop. Orion shut the door behind us. I suddenly felt trapped in a room with two dangerous creatures I knew nothing about. I pulled free of Azrael's grasp and stepped away from him. They looked so human and acted so normal. How could they be Immortals? My fingers gripped the edge of the counter.

Orion furrowed his brow and folded his arms across his bulky frame. "Great way to break it to her easy."

"How was I to know that human would try to attack me?" Azrael drew the curtains over the windows, making the room dark like a dungeon.

I couldn't tear my gaze away from Azrael. His chest flashed like perfect marble between the slash in his tunic from his shoulder all the way to his hip.

Orion narrowed his eyes. "What're we goin' to do with Aura now that she knows our secret? You know the High Druid of Fire is going to be furious."

Azrael shook his head like he didn't know what to do.

Orion blocked the door. "We have to find some way to shut her up. You know what could happen if even more people find out we're Immortals."

I took a step back. This wasn't good. "What are you going to do to me now that I know your secret?" I tried to sound brave, but they were Immortals. I couldn't fight them and I certainly couldn't outrun them.

Azrael turned toward me and slowly approached with his hands up. "Don't be afraid, Aura. We're not going to hurt you. We've been more than careful this whole time. We promise to be on our best behavior."

"You don't know how hard that's been," Orion mumbled darkly.

Azrael continued to take slow, deliberate steps toward me.

I held my breath and gripped the pommel of the sword Azrael had given me. I swallowed several times to be sure my voice wouldn't shake. "Stop, Azrael." I lifted the sword and pointed the tip at his chest. "Stay where you are."

Orion laughed. "See, Azrael—I told you she would think you were a monster. We're too different from her. She's been living like a human her whole life. She doesn't know anything about our Neviahan culture or people. She doesn't even know why she should or shouldn't be afraid of us."

My sword was useless against him, but Azrael respectfully took a step back. "Please, Aura, let us explain what we are."

Orion advanced toward me. "It would be easier if we tied her up and just took her to the sanctuary. 'Tis too complicated to explain, and we'll just end up scaring her more."

I turned and pointed the sword at Orion. He vanished and then appeared in the corner of the room, holding my sword.

"That's not funny," Azrael scolded. "Don't you remember how fragile mortals are? You could have ripped her arm off running that fast."

Orion didn't look sympathetic.

Azrael held out his hand. "Sit down and talk with us, Aura," he offered.

I balled my hands into fists at my sides and stood my ground. I didn't know if I should be afraid or amazed, but my heart was aching. I had just started to fall in love with Azrael. He actually had me believing that we could one day have a life together if I chose him over Lucas.

The image of me, old and gray, standing next to Azrael, who would be still just as beautiful, young, and strong pierced my mind. Liquid pain burned in my eyes as I stared at him. I blinked several times, refusing to cry over my own foolishness.

Azrael let out a surrendering sigh when I didn't take his hand. He slid a stool to the counter and sat down. "What Ruburt said about us being Immortals 'tis true. I was born in 1057 as a mortal. I started my Watcher training when I was only twelve. When I was twenty-four, the King of Neviah granted me immortality so I could stay on Earth and fight the Rebellion until Erebus is destroyed."

I glanced at Orion in the corner of the room. He still had his arms crossed, and my sword was propped against the wall. They had immortal speed and strength. That's how Azrael was able to catch me so fast when I fell off my horse. That's why I never saw them eat or sleep. Orion could probably chop down a mighty oak with just one swing of his massive battle axe. Everything made sense now.

Azrael narrowed his eyes and stared at me as if reading my thoughts. "Our bodies are different from yours, but I promise you, our hearts and Neviahan souls are still the same."

I nodded to the cot where Korban lay. "Why was Korban hurt?" I asked, trying to make sense of the Immortals' strengths and weaknesses.

"We will never die of old age or illness," Azrael answered. "But there are a few things that can hurt an Immortal. Starfire is one of them. There are enemies that can destroy even an Immortal Watcher. Shadow Lords can kill Immortals."

"Only if they stab us in the heart," Orion amended.

Azrael nodded and continued, "Since Korban wasn't stabbed in the heart and he didn't feel the full force of Starfire, his body has gone into survival sleep until he heals."

Orion fumbled with a smithing hammer in his hands. "The longest anyone has ever slept is forty-eight years."

"Forty-eight years?" I hoped Korban didn't take that long to recover. "I'm not an Immortal, and I can't afford to wait another week like you can, let alone years." I didn't hide the panic in my voice. My time on Earth was only temporary. I had to do what I was sent down here to do before my time was up.

Azrael threw Orion a warning glare. "That Watcher had both his arms ripped off. It took forty-eight years for everything to grow back." Azrael turned toward me and relaxed his expression. His voice filled with compassion. "Don't worry, Aura. Korban's injury wasn't nearly as severe. He will awaken any day now."

I watched Korban's motionless body, hoping he would awaken now. Azrael caught my attention again. "Korban will be fine. We are different from mortal Watchers, like you," he said. "The strength of our bodies and powers are increased. We are over a hundred times faster and stronger."

I didn't feel as afraid since Azrael was voluntarily giving me more information, but my heart still ached for the loss of our potential romantic relationship. Perhaps this was a sign that Lucas and I were supposed to be together.

I sat at the table across from Azrael. "How many Immortals are there?"

Azrael looked to Orion for an answer. Orion shrugged. "I don't know."

"The twelve High Druid Neviahans are Immortal," Azrael said. "John and Enoch are Immortal."

"So are the three Nephites," Orion added.

"No one knows for sure," Azrael said. "There are probably hundreds of Immortals who get to stay on Earth until Erebus is defeated. We each have a role to play in this battle and the twelve High Druids send us Watchers on quests wherever heroes are needed."

Orion relaxed and leaned against the counter where we sat. "Some Watchers have been fighting Erebus for over a thousand years."

The thought of battling the Shadow Legion for a thousand years exhausted me.

"I know 'tis a lot to take in," Azrael said. "I don't want you to be afraid of us. I will tell you all you want to know."

I wasn't afraid anymore, but my mind filled with more questions about my culture and identity. "Outside our human bodies, do Neviahans look different from humans?" I imagined the most alien creature I had ever seen. Some sailors had brought a giant squid to a festival in London a few years ago. I'd never seen anything so strange.

"Oh, yes! We look very different from humans," Azrael answered.

I clenched my hands together as panic flooded me. I was probably a hideous creature in a human body. "I don't have tentacles, do I?"

Azrael and Orion froze in place. Orion's eyes went wide. Azrael studied my face. Then they both erupted in robust laughter.

"No, no, no." Azrael shook his head. "We have a human-like form, but we're taller, much stronger, and we radiate Neviahan light. Remember how your skin looked when you created Starfire?"

I faintly remembered my skin glowing with pure light energy. I nodded.

"'Tis what we look like," he said. "Humans who have seen us in our Neviahan form sometimes call us angels, or gods."

I remembered the paintings of mighty archangels on the cathedral walls. "That doesn't sound so bad."

Azrael leaned forward, his eyes wide with resolute promise. "Trust me, Auriella—you are the most beautiful creature in the Kingdom of Neviah. Here on Earth, your pure spirit radiates past your human façade. You are a beautiful woman both on Earth and in Neviah."

I paused and tried to shake off his flattery with curiosity. "How are Neviahans born?" I blushed at my own question. "I mean, how do people like us get to Earth?"

Azrael shrugged. "Just like everyone else. We are born into human bodies and give them life. We don't steal human bodies like the Shadow Legion. The humans are able to raise us until we are ready to fight the Rebellion."

My brow creased. "What about eating? I've never seen you eat."

Orion cracked a wry half smile and said, "Since we are Immortal, we won't starve to death if we stop eatin'. We haven't eaten much on this trip. We've been saving all our rations for you."

I softened my stance and relaxed my tense arms.

Orion gave me a soft smile. "When we're not travelin', we enjoy a good meal every once in a while. Why would we want to give up sweet, juicy apples, seasoned bread soaked with warm butter, and rosemary grilled potatoes?" Orion reached into his pack and pulled out several apricots and handed one to me and one to Azrael.

"Thank you." I waited until they started eating before I took a bite. I actually concentrated on enjoying the taste instead of eating just for the sake of nourishment. The sweet fruit flowed through my mouth and down my throat.

"Food is not just for survival," Azrael said. "It brings people together and can actually be quite enjoyable. We get a small amount of energy from food, but most of our energy comes from our elemental sources."

"Like how the sun gives me extra energy?"

"Exactly," Azrael said. "But as Immortals, we depend on our energy sources much more." He set the apricot pit on the table and Orion held out his hand. The seed burst to life and sprouted into a tender young sapling. Perfect leaves fanned open and emerald light showered around it. Orion's eyes glistened like jade stones as he used his powers.

"Amazing!" I placed my seed next to Azrael's and watched Orion intertwine the two tiny trees together until they formed one tree.

Orion gave me a satisfied smile. "It doesn't matter how strong a person is," he said. "We are stronger when we work together."

Azrael lifted his gaze to meet mine. "After Korban awakens, it will take all four of us to defeat Erebus."

I shook my head. "But I'm not as strong as you, and I can't control Starfire."

Azrael reached for my hand. "I wasn't flattering you when I told the slave master you are the strongest warrior."

I pulled away from him and stared at his perfect strong hands, then gazed into his glittering eyes. I didn't dare touch him. It would be like touching a timeless angel from the heavens, and my heart would only break more knowing I couldn't be with him.

Azrael would live on as an Immortal, and I would grow old and die. Is this why he kept his secret from me? He knew all along we couldn't be together. Was winning my affection just a game to him?

I looked away, and he slid his hand over mine. I froze as he spoke. "I love you, Aura. My feelings for you haven't changed." A breeze blew a lock of hair over my shoulder. "I am completely dedicated to you for all of my immortal life on Earth, and I want you by my side for all of my eternal Neviahan existence."

I still couldn't look at him. Why was he doing this to me? Why was he setting us up for tragedy?

Another phantom breeze ran through my hair and lingered like a kiss on my cheek. It felt so real. I raise my hand to my face to hold the sensation there. "Wind," I realized, and turned back to Azrael. "Your power is the wind element."

Azrael nodded. A gust swirled through the enclosed room and blew the fire from the lamps in the shop. I just knew Azrael grinned at me in the darkness like a mischievous bandit. Using my power, I lifted my hand and the lamps blazed back to life.

I stared at Azrael in the lamp-lit room. My breath quickened as I allowed myself to get lost in his silver eyes sparkling behind his mask.

Warm wind danced around me, making my hair look like living fire.

"Even the shadows flee from the light of a single flame." Azrael touched my fingertips with his. Silver sparks skittered up my arm and filled me with celestial energy. "Our time on Earth is only temporary, but I will love you for eternity."

Chapter Fourteen

Wedding Gift

I put my hands on my hips and playfully narrowed my eyes. "Now I know why you are some of the most frustrating and reckless men I have ever met."

Azrael and Orion laughed as if taking my declaration as a compliment.

"We weren't supposed to tell you about our immortality," Orion said. "Once we defeat Erebus, we will take you to the sanctuary. Zacaris, the high druid of the Northern Sanctuary, was suppose to explain all this to you."

I thought about my commitment to go with them to the sanctuary. It weighed on my mind like an unpaid debt. There were many problems waiting for me when I got back home. Lucas and I had to convince the king to give the Scottish their independence, I had a wedding to postpone, and then there was the threat of Erebus and the Shadow Legion. "We don't have much time." I twisted my hair nervously around my shoulder. What if Erebus was already in London and Lucas was fighting him alone?" The only thing that comforted me was knowing that Lucas had my ruby necklace. It could heal him as he fought and help him survive the Legion's attacks.

I knelt next to Korban's cot. "Come on, Korban," I whispered. "We need you to wake up." I brushed his hair back. Hot white sparks skittered from my fingers across his face. I gasped and jerked away.

"Aye," Korban moaned.

"Korban?" I leaned over the cot.

He put his hand over his brow.

"Finally," Orion breathed.

I leaned closer, but was careful not to touch him. "Korban, say something," I begged.

Korban moaned, then said, "You sure know how to throw a punch, Aura."

Azrael and Orion burst out laughing.

I didn't think it was funny. "Are you hurt?" I pressed.

Korban sat up. "I'm great, actually. I feel like I have more energy now than the last few times I've awoken from survival sleep."

Orion crossed his burly arms. "'Tis about time you got your lazy butt out of bed."

"Aye." Korban shook his head. "You know it takes me a while to recover from elemental strikes. That hit would've killed me if I were mortal." He met my eyes and covered his mouth.

"'Tis all right," Azrael said. "We already told her we are Immortals."

Korban lowered his hand. "Zacaris isn't going to be happy with you. He has that step-by-step training program, and the lesson on Immortals isn't until lesson thirteen."

"When do you think you will be able to travel?" Azrael asked. "A battle in London awaits us."

"Maybe tonight." Korban stumbled to his feet. "Don't worry about me. The one we should be worried about is the mortal." He nodded toward me.

"I can make it," I assured. "I'm pretty tough for a mortal."

Korban stretched his neck to one side. "No kidding."

"What about sleep?" Orion asked.

"I promise I won't fall off my horse," I said before he could say it.

"There's no time to lose," Azrael said. "I need to find Baby, and then we should pack and leave right away."

"You should get a leash for that cat, Azrael," Korban teased.

Azrael shook his head. "He's probably sleeping off a good meal. Hopefully he didn't eat anyone's livestock again."

Azrael and I both reached for the handle on the door. A purple spark jumped from my hand to his.

I pulled away and ignored the illumination. It struck me with wonder every time our energy connected. I couldn't allow this connection to influence my feelings for him. The worst sin I ever committed was momentarily falling in love with an Immortal. I wasn't going to let it happen again. "I won't need an escort," I said coolly. "Just meet me at Ruburt's house in an hour."

I lifted my skirt and rushed down the narrow road to Ruburt's cottage. As I neared, I lowered my gaze and slowed my pace.

Ruburt was outside, bent over, working in his garden at the edge of the meadow. He straightened when he saw me.

"Korban is awake." It took all my strength to hold back the flood of emotion and worry inside me.

"You don't seem too happy 'bout it," Ruburt noted.

I took a deep breath. "I'm happy he's awake." I focused on my horse grazing in the meadow. "After the battle in London, I will leave for the Watcher sanctuary. I may never see you again."

Ruburt gave me a soft smile. "You have a great destiny, Lady Auriella. Don't let anything hold you back or distract you from your mission."

I couldn't help but think about my greatest distraction—Lucas. "Do you think Lucas will come with me?" I asked.

"Of course he will."

The sunlight danced off the straw rooftop of Ruburt's tiny cottage, making it glitter like gold. Tall meadow grass swayed around me. "I don't want to leave England," I muttered.

Ruburt leaned against his shovel like a walking stick as we made our way to the cottage. "This is only the beginning of your journey, Auriella. I don't think you should live in human society any longer. One of your greatest weaknesses is that you get too attached to us humans."

"What?" I asked, shocked and confused by what he was telling me. "I love being with people. It's all I've ever known."

"You will still be with people," Ruburt said. "Just people like you. Think of how much you can learn from them. They live in a completely Neviahan society. But. . ." Ruburt held up one finger and cautioned, "If you go with the Neviahans to the sanctuary, they will train you in combat. For the rest of your life, you will constantly battle the darkness. Is this the life you want?"

I thought about Ruburt's warning. Even if I lived the rest of my life in a human society, pretending to be a human, the Rebellion would still hunt me. I narrowed my eyes resolutely. I couldn't ever stop fighting. "You already know what I'm going to choose, don't you?" I asked Ruburt.

Ruburt chuckled. "Of course. I know the prophecy of the Lady of Neviah, but I also know you, Auriella. Do you remember when Cassi was trapped in Hazella's magical cage?"

I nodded.

"You could've easily run away on your own and escaped from the witch, but you didn't. You endured until you found a way to save us all."

I took a deep breath and banished my fears.

Ruburt shrugged. "Besides, it's not like you won't ever come back. The Watchers are always on missions. As soon as your training is complete, the druids will assign you to new areas of the world."

I lifted my gaze and dried my wet eyelashes. "Do you remember the library in Oswestry?"

Ruburt nodded. "Yes. Your favorite books were about geography."

"I might get to see all those places. What if I get to be Egypt's new Watcher? Do you think I could live in a pyramid? I would also love to stand at the base of the mountains in China." I clasped my hands together and spun on the ball of one foot in a dance. "I can't wait to finish my combat training and fight the Rebellion around the world."

Ruburt laughed. "Then there's no time to lose." He opened the door to the cottage and followed me inside. Pearl helped me pack a few necessary items while Ruburt watched through the window for the Immortals. "It looks like a storm's comin' in," he said.

Pearl handed me another bag and an extra quilt while escorting me out the door to my waiting horse. "Take care of yourself and make sure you stay warm. Just because those boys can't catch cold doesn't mean you won't. Drink lots of water and don't forget to eat. I know how you forget to take care of yourself when you have your mind set on something."

I held the bundle close to my chest. "Thank you, Pearl."

Hooves thundered from down the road as the other three Neviahans approached. "It's time," Ruburt said. His voice strained to hold back emotion.

I hugged the dwarf family goodbye, possibly for the last time, memorizing their faces and imprinting the memory of them forever in my mind.

I threw my leg over my mare, gripped the reins, and turned toward the Immortals.

"Come on, Auriella," Korban said. "Let's go send some demons back to Hell."

"Hazzah!" Ruburt shouted and raised his fist in the air.

"Hazzah!" We shouted in return.

The horses pawed the road. The sky grew darker. An icy bite whipped through the wind. Baby eyed the storm and let out a low growl. The Rebellion's dark storm was a reminder that we were still being hunted.

We turned our horses and galloped into the shroud toward London.

We rode through the night that seemed to never end. Enough time had passed I knew it should be morning, but no sun broke through Erebus's black storm. My stomach tightened as London appeared on the horizon. The king would be furious when I returned empty handed. The only thing of value I gained from this trip was learning that the Scottish were not the enemies. I had no idea how many Legionnaires waited for me, or if Lucas was still alive. I didn't know how I would tell him I lost my engagement ring.

I glanced at Azrael, who flashed me a perfect, charming smile—I didn't know how to explain that problem, either. I knew I had to find a way to get the king to pull our military out of Scotland, I had to destroy Erebus, and then convince Lucas to come to the sanctuary with me.

We stopped at the edge of London and braced ourselves for whatever lay beyond the gates. I flexed my feet back in the stirrups to stretch my aching legs, and watched the sweat drip off my horse onto the dusty road in large drops.

Azrael turned to Baby and instructed, "Make your way to the castle. Don't let anyone see you." Baby nodded and bounded into the forest. "I should ride in first. It may be a trap."

"It's best if I lead," I suggested. "My people know me."

Azrael hesitated, then nodded in agreement.

We rode through the streets of London toward the stables by the main castle courtyard. No squires rushed to help us dismount. Something was wrong.

Korban flung himself from his horse and unsheathed his blades. He sniffed the air. "I can smell them. They're here."

Azrael held my waist and helped me from my horse. I allowed him to be a gentleman, but I wasn't going to spend any more time fantasizing about a romantic relationship with him. "Stay focused," I said more for my own benefit and then stepped away from Azrael. "We need to speak with Lucas and tell him about the Shadow Legion's plans to take over London."

Azrael took my hand and pulled me to his chest.

Irritation and anger scorched inside me. Why was Azrael torturing me like this, making me hope for an impractical relationship with him? I lowered my head and forced my body to go rigid in his arms. I had to see Lucas soon before I fell completely for Azrael and all three of us ended up with broken hearts.

Azrael smiled mischievously. "Lucas won't think highly of me once he learns I plan on stealing you away from him."

"Stop it, Azrael," I nearly growled. "You're being arrogant now."

Azrael shook his head and let me go. "I'm not arrogant, just determined. You still have a choice, and I'm feeling confident."

The breath escaped my lungs at his boldness. He was really making me angry.

Sunlight momentarily broke through the black storm and streaked through the stable windows. My skin sparkled in the brief ray of light. Azrael put his hand to his chest. He appreciated my Lifelight in a way no human could. I allowed myself to get lost in the depths of his eyes.

"Auriella!" I recognized the voice immediately.

"Lucas." I whirled around and watched Lucas bound through the stable doors. He slid to a stop and froze in place, eyeing Azrael, Orion, and Korban. "You brought back barbarians?" His face wrinkled in disgust. He marched toward me and yanked me away from them. "I guess this means you didn't complete your assassination mission?" he chided.

"No." I shook my head and tried not to feel hurt at this cold homecoming. Lucas shrugged away from me. Wasn't he just as happy to see me safely home as I was to see him alive and well?

Lucas narrowed his eyes. "You failed, Auriella."

"Lucas, listen to me," I begged. Lucas still held my wrist, but at least he seemed attentive. "Let's put aside all prejudices and talk about the real threat for one moment. You have no idea what I've been through in the last week. The Shadow Legion is here. We need to meet with the king and warn him," I said.

"The king is preoccupied," Lucas said without emotion.

"Lucas, it's important."

He glared at me. "Right now, I'm the only one allowed to meet with the king. It's for his own protection."

I tried not to sound disappointed. "He's not seeing anyone else?"

Lucas shook his head.

It didn't matter, as long as Lucas was willing to listen to me and report my findings to the king. "Tell him we need to pull our military out of Scotland."

Lucas looked at Azrael with narrowed eyes, then back to me. "Did your barbarian friends tell you this?"

I twisted my wrist and broke from his grip. It wasn't Lucas's fault he didn't understand. If he got to know the Scottish, he would see we were more alike than different. "They saved my life. Don't you care about that?"

"Auriella," Lucas said with more gentleness. His cold fingers brushed past my cheek. Finally, I was getting through to him. "I love you," he said. I smiled and started to melt, but then his face twisted into a scowl. "But I will not thank a barbarian, not even for saving the life of my fiancée." Lucas turned to Azrael and spat on the ground.

"Lucas!" His words hurt worse than a slap to the face.

Lucas turned to Azrael, Orion, and Korban. "A life for a life. You saved my fiancée and I will allow you to leave my kingdom with your heads. Don't return, or I will withdraw that promise." Lucas must've known I wouldn't leave with him willingly, so he scooped me up in his arms and carried me toward the castle.

I looked over Lucas's shoulder and met Azrael's gaze. I shook my head and mouthed the words, "I'm sorry." I didn't fight Lucas. At least this way, I could argue with him in private.

Lucas walked through the courtyard and into the castle before he started talking again. "Pulling our troops out of Scotland is a horrible idea. As soon as we stop exercising military authority, they will rebel and rise up against us. They're terrorists, Auriella. We have to keep them under our control."

"No, Lucas, we don't." I tried not to sound emotional. "The Scottish can control themselves. They have a perfectly capable monarchy set up and the people are happy with their culture and way of life. We are invading their land and taking their goods."

Lucas sputtered. "We're not stealing from them. We're taxing them."

"By killing their men and raping their women?" I writhed from his arms and forced him to set me down.

"All lies. Our military is protecting them," Lucas explained. "We only tax them for what we need to support our military. Do you know how much war costs?"

"Yes, war costs many lives. You of all people should know this." Lucas opened his mouth, but I stopped him. "Listen to me, Lucas. We are focusing on a threat that doesn't exist when the real threat is right here in our own country. The threat is from the diplomats running the government. The terrorists are already here and using our own government to destroy us."

I caught my breath. "You say we are trying to help other countries, but how can we help other countries if we can't take care of ourselves?"

Lucas snatched my hand in a crushing grip and led me to my bedroom chamber. "We are improving the Scottish way of life."

"No, the English are destroying their way of life." I tried to pull away, but to no avail. "Our culture is not like theirs, but that doesn't give us the right to go in and change them."

"But what about the children who are starving in Scotland?" Lucas baited.

I pried his fingers one by one from my arm. "What about the starving children in England? Why are we spending ridiculous amount of money on foreign wars when England has so many problems on home soil?"

Lucas slammed his fist into the wall. The stone cracked under his hand. His fingers didn't even redden from the blow. I took a step back to avoid his outburst of anger.

The magic necklace I realized. It made him strong and nearly indestructible, perhaps the power was too much for him and that's why he was acting this way.

I wasn't going to let him intimidate me. "We need to bring our military home," I said. "If any land needs protecting from terrorists, it's ours."

Lucas tightened his jaw. "Are you talking about Erebus and the Shadow Legion?"

I nodded.

Lucas rolled his eyes. "The Dark Rebellion isn't infiltrating our government. We are too strong. The whole time you were gone, there were no disturbances, not one sighting of even a Shadow Spirit. The maids were happy they didn't have to clean up any of your messes."

I pressed my lips into a thin line and stepped into my bedroom. "I thought you would believe me." I took in several quick breaths, trying to suppress my emotions. "Leave, Lucas. I can't talk to you right now. I'm too upset."

Lucas whirled around and slammed the door behind him as he left. I fell on my bed and buried my face in my pillow. This was the worst thing that could have happened. Lucas was angry with me, and I hated that I was angry with him. We were best friends and we used to be able to work anything out.

It would be harder losing Lucas this way than losing him to war. I put my fingertips to my mouth and took in several quick breaths. Why couldn't Lucas at least try to see things from my perspective? He had been so different since his return. If war changed his heart into something cold, hopefully my love could heal him.

I stood and walked through the balcony doors.

The world was completely dark, No sun, no moon, no stars. I couldn't tell what time it was or even if it was day or night.

A few lamps came from the city below, but most of the light was from the single torch hanging on the wall of my bedroom.

The fire light danced off my arm over the scars where the venom was drained. Right now was probably a bad time to ask Lucas where he had gotten the poison. He couldn't have known it would attract the Shadow Wolves or he would have never given it to me.

A breeze caught my hair and tousled it like scarlet streamers. I turned back to my room, pulled out a fresh dress from the wardrobe, and laid it on the bed. I wadded my bathrobe in my arms and trudged down the hall to the washroom. I couldn't help but be annoyed that the seamstress still hadn't replaced the curtains. She probably figured no one would be peeping into the window on the second story of the castle or it was her way of punishing me for destroying another set.

Too exhausted to use my powers, I pulled several buckets of hot water from the pot over the fire and poured them into the bath until the water was warm. I peeled off my well-traveled clothes and slipped into the tub. Closing my eyes, I tried not to think about anything, especially not about my fight with Lucas.

My mind swam with memories of the last two weeks. So much had changed. Lucas was back from the dead and we were engaged. I'd met three other Watchers, traveled across the country as an assassin, and returned as a diplomat—a diplomat no one believed. All the muscles in my back tightened from stress.

I couldn't help but wonder if the power from the necklace was making Lucas act like a power-hungry tyrant. I didn't regret giving it to him. It probably saved his life, but I had to get it back before it completely destroyed him.

Then there was Azrael. No matter what happened between Lucas and I, Azrael would be there. It wasn't fair to marry Lucas when I loved Azrael as much as I did. I had to find a way not to love Azrael anymore. I sank further into the water.

"Hello?" Lucas's voice came from behind me.

I whirled around and ducked low in the water. The waves bounced off the sides of the tub and slapped against my back. "Lucas?" I whispered, and didn't hide my horror. "I'm naked."

Lucas closed the door behind him. "I know."

"You shouldn't be in here right now," I scolded.

"I couldn't wait any longer to talk to you."

"Turn around," I demanded.

Lucas dropped his shoulders and turned around. I noticed the bouquet of roses he hid behind his back.

I jumped out of the tub and wrapped my robe around myself without drying off. The fabric clung to my wet legs and back. I took a deep breath and crossed my arms. "You better have a good reason for coming in here."

Lucas faced me. "I do." His jaw tightened as he held out the flowers. "I'm in love with you." He stepped closer, but I didn't take the bouquet.

I gripped my robe tighter across my chest. "What about our fight?"

"I've thought about what you said, and I'm sorry for how I acted." I allowed Lucas to take my hand. He fingered where my engagement ring should have been.

I bowed my head repentantly. "I lost the ring."

"Don't worry, it's just a ring," Lucas said sweetly and pushed the flowers into my hand. "I'm just happy you're home. I want you as my queen, and no one else." The candles in the room flickered. I bent down and took in the scent of roses. "If you will marry me, then as a wedding present, I will pull all the troops out of Scotland."

A smile escaped my lips. "Really? You can do that?"

"Yes, my lady." Lucas bent low and kissed my hand.

I could save countless people by marrying him. I had the power to stop a war. After that, we could focus our military strength on destroying the real threat, the Shadow Legion.

Lucas stroked my face with the back of his fingers. "The king would like to honor our engagement with a feast tonight."

All I had to do was marry Lucas and there would be peace between Scotland and England. I swallowed hard and looked into his hungry eyes. But if I married him, would there ever be peace in my heart?

Chapter Fifteen

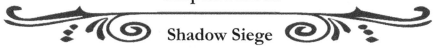

Shadow Siege

Lucas wasted no time getting me a new engagement ring. The band of blue sapphires glinted off my left hand and stood out against the burgundy and black lace dress I wore. Lucas had gotten me a black feathered mask for the ball. I always disliked masquerades, but now I hated them even more as the masks reminded me of Azrael and the curse I would never break.

Even though no one had seen any rebels since I left, I kept a vigilant watch as we walked through the crowd to the king's table. The nobles danced and feasted as the musicians played.

"Relax." Lucas squeezed my hand. "You could at least smile like you are happy to be engaged."

I dropped my shoulders and forced a smile, but part of me still hoped to see Azrael in the crowd.

Lucas led me to the seats next to the king, where we sat as the guests of honor. I tried to be happy that I was engaged to the boy I had loved since I was a child, but so much sorrow clouded my weak façade.

Luckily, Lucas sat between the king and me. Despite the barrier, I reminded myself to try to get along with King Edward. "Thank you for hosting this celebration in our honor," I said to him.

The king did not reply. His head hung low as he stared into a glass of wine. Death itself painted his face. He glanced at me with dark, hollow eyes. Something was wrong with him. His pupils had dilated so wide, there was no color left. "Your Majesty," I asked. "Are you ill?"

Lucas gave my hand a reassuring squeeze. "Don't worry about him. He's drunk."

I had seen him drunk before, but this was different. I swallowed hard. At least he was in no condition to chide me about my failed mission.

I watched the crowd dance in a hypnotizing rhythm. Each guest seemed jubilant and relaxed as if they didn't have a care in the world.

This didn't make sense. Erebus's black storm still ominously covered the sky, but no one had seen any Shadow Rebels.

Lucas slid a glass of wine to me. "Drink. It will help you relax. You worry too much."

I fingered the stem of the goblet and glanced at the king. Seeing someone that drunk made me never want to put that poison to my lips. It reminded me of the Shadow venom. "Lucas?" I started. "Where did you get the poison you gave me before I left?"

Lucas took a long drink, then casually shrugged. "I got it from a gypsy merchant on my way back from the crusades. I thought it might come in handy someday."

"Oh," I replied. It made sense. I decided not to tell him it was really a venomous lure. He would be overwhelmed with guilt if he knew he put me in danger. I traced the scars on my arm where the wolf bit me, then fidgeted with the fringe of the table-cloth. It looked like England really didn't need me anymore. I had to find a way to ask Lucas to come with me to the sanctuary after we pulled the English troops out of Scotland.

Lucas put his cold hand over mine, withdrawing me out of my thoughts. "You aren't drinking."

"I'm not thirsty." I shied away from his touch. It was wrong, but I couldn't help compare it to Azrael's warm touch and the way our celestial energy collided, as if connecting us together.

I had to forget about Azrael or I would be miserable being married to Lucas.

I glanced up and saw the familiar god-like Neviahan. The crowd parted for him as he walked toward me with a confident stride. His magnificent eyes sparkled from behind the mask.

"Azrael?" I whispered to myself, horrified that he had the nerve to show up at my engagement celebration. I turned to Lucas and smiled pleasantly. "Excuse me." I left the table before Lucas could ask why then followed Azrael into a private corner. "What are you doing here?" I whispered coarsely.

Azrael shrugged nonchalantly. "Following the plan."

I narrowed my eyes. "What plan?"

He smiled even wider. "The plan we came up with after Lucas kidnapped you."

"Ah!" I pressed my palm against my forehead. "Azrael, I wasn't kidnapped."

Azrael smiled smugly and nodded. "It sure looked like it to us."

Another song started, and before I could react, Azrael gripped my hand and waist. He spun me onto the dance floor and ignored my momentary lack of grace. "You look beautiful," he said as if continuing a casual conversation.

I couldn't help but smile whenever he smiled. "The dress looks beautiful," I corrected.

He leaned forward. His lips brushed across my ear. "No, you look beautiful."

Waves of emotion flooded me. I was so in love with him, and it terrified me. "Azrael," I hesitated. "You really shouldn't be dancing with me," I said through my teeth. I could feel people staring at us. "I don't belong to you." It didn't feel right saying that, so I amended, "You have my heart, but not my hand." I desperately wished that Azrael was mortal so we at least had a chance of being together.

Azrael grinned, making his eyes shimmer past his mask. My breath escaped me. "You shouldn't be dancing with me."

Azrael raised one eyebrow. "What?" he asked with false innocence. "Lucas can't handle a little competition?"

"Azrael," I whispered. My voice strained. I could feel my heart breaking. I had to marry Lucas. It was the only way I could stop the war. "I'm already engaged." I tried not to sound bitter.

The statement didn't shake him. "Engaged in what?"

There was no use in arguing with him. "Have you seen any Shadow Spirits or Shadow Lords since you've been here?"

Azrael nodded. He stepped closer to me and whispered, "Over a hundred."

My eyes went wide as horror gripped my stomach. "How can that be? Lucas said they hadn't—."

Azrael cut me off. "Erebus is here too. Korban and Orion are in the castle tracking him."

My heart raced. "The Shadow King is in the castle?"

"Shhh," Azrael whispered.

I pressed my lips together and looked around the room. "Where is your cat?"

Azrael smirked and pointed to one of the tables. A long, striped tail swooshed back and forth from under the tablecloth.

I tried not to laugh. "If people see him, they are going to think all Scots are terrorists. Which reminds me, Lucas agreed to pull all the troops out of Scotland if I marry him." I forced myself to smile. "I can bring peace between the two countries and we can focus on the real battle against the Rebellion."

Azrael didn't look happy, but kept his voice regal and calm. "Is that the only reason why you are marrying Lucas?"

I dropped my shoulders. "What else am I supposed to do, Azrael?"

"Don't," Azrael said. "Don't sacrifice yourself by marrying him."

I stared into his perfect immortal eyes, and for a wonderful, brief moment, imagined myself marrying him instead of Lucas.

Whitened knuckles gripped Azrael's shoulder. "May I cut in?" Lucas asked.

"You already have," Azrael murmured. His eyes narrowed. He turned to me and mouthed the words, "Stay on guard."

Lucas slipped one hand behind my waist. "Bold fellow, isn't he?"

I nodded in agreement. "Yes, he is." A smile escaped my lips. I loved that about Azrael.

Lucas and I danced to several songs without speaking to each other. I didn't know what to say to him. Doubt over whether I was doing the right thing by marrying him preoccupied my mind. The songs seemed to drag on and as soon as one ended, Lucas held me tighter and forced me to dance another one with him. I shouldn't be dancing with him or anyone right now.

Korban and Orion were navigating the halls, doing my duty while I wasted time dancing. I couldn't shake the uneasy feeling knotting inside me.

"You are simply ravishing," Lucas flattered, interrupting my thoughts.

I looked up. "Thank you, m'lord." Movement from the ceiling caught my attention. Shadows in the silhouettes of men moved along the beams, then seeped into the stones.

Lucas looked behind him. "What are you looking at? Is something wrong?"

I shook my head. "Excuse me. I need to check on something." I pulled away from his grip and raced from the ballroom and up a flight of stairs to find the rebels.

I rounded the corner into a heated battle. Korban whirled his swords in a dance of blurred blades and slammed his weapons into a Shadow Lord. The Legionnaire crumbled and hit the floor.

Ash of dead Shadow Legionnaires carpeted the ground. Orion held his axe and charged into several Shadow Lords like a massive plow. A gangly Shadow Lord dropped from the ceiling behind Korban. I shot a stream of fire from my fingertips and disintegrated the devilish creature.

Korban whirled around as the rebel fell in a heap of ash. "Well struck, my lady," he said. He crossed his weapons and sliced into another decrepit Shadow Lord. Even in the narrow hall, Korban seemed to dance with his weapons. Shadow blood smudged across his bare chest and leather war kilt. His swords whirled fluidly around him like a slicing shield, moving with the tempo of the music from the celebration. He cut through the charging line of Shadow Lords as gracefully as the nobles dancing below. He spun with the blades, creating a metallic chorus to the traditional folk songs. I could clearly see his gift with weapons.

The song ended and Korban cut through the last attacking Shadow Lord.

The main hall erupted in applause as if for Korban's epic victory. I couldn't help but clap too after seeing the magnificent weapon display.

Korban didn't hold back his smile.

Orion approached me and rested his massive axe casually on his shoulder. He let out a long whistle. "I thought you were stunnin' before, but you clean up good."

I curtsied in my ball gown. "You clean up good as well." I put my hands on my hips and nodded toward the pile of ash.

Orion laughed and flexed his bulging chest muscles.

I instantly blushed and covered my eyes. "Orion, I'm an English lady."

"And we're Scottish barbarians," Orion chortled.

Azrael's voice came from behind, "This way." I whirled around to face the Immortal I loved more than I should. At least Azrael was still dressed like a gentleman or I might have fainted seeing his bare chest and leather battle kilt. "Baby picked up Erebus's scent."

I lifted my flowing gown and raced with my beautiful, immortal barbarian comrades down the hallway. "How did you get Baby out of the ballroom without anyone seeing him?" I asked Azrael. The cat was the size of a small horse and filled the width of the hallway.

"Lucas ended the feast after the last dance. While everyone was focused on him we slipped out." Azrael said then added, "I don't think he's happy you left the celebration."

I bit my lip. How was I going to explain this to Lucas?

Baby bounded through a doorway. He froze in an aggressive stance and let out a low growl.

Azrael drew his sword. "That is it," he said. "'Tis the room where Erebus has been hiding."

I scanned the room and shook my head. There had to be some kind of mistake. "Azrael, this is my bedroom."

Korban shifted his weight and I heard Orion swallow.

Azrael reached for my hand, his eyes wide with alarm. "Aura, you're the target."

"See, I told you she would make great bait," Korban said, catching his breath.

"Why?" I asked. "Wouldn't the king be a more likely target?"

Azrael ignored my question and paced the room. "This isn't good. 'Tis very bad."

Korban dropped his arms to his sides, making his swords clang together. "I will just say what's on everyone's mind—Shadow Queen."

Orion jerked. His face turned white.

"Shadow Queen?" I asked. "Who is that?"

Azrael continued to pace. "'Tis a Shadow Lord's mate. All the women who rebelled from the kingdom of Neviah lost their creation abilities when the King of Neviah turned them into Shadows. They lost the ability to have children. A Shadow Lord can't breed with humans. If he is going to create his own race of demonic offspring, he needs to find a true Neviahan woman to be his mate, one who still has the Lifelight."

I froze, trying to process what Azrael was saying.

Korban continued, "He needs to find a Neviahan woman who will willingly marry him and give birth to his offspring. The only Neviahan woman here is you Aura. You're the target."

I slapped my hand over my mouth to keep from gasping. It was the most horrible thing I had ever heard. Why would I, or any Neviahan woman, willingly do such a thing?

"Where's Lucas?" Azrael asked. "He might be in trouble."

My hands trembled. "The last time I saw him, he was at the feast."

"Baby and I will check the king's chamber," Azrael said. "Orion and Korban, search the main hall."

The three Neviahan men ran off in opposite directions down the hallway.

I couldn't just stay here and wait if Lucas was in trouble. Gripping my sword, I raced down the hallway toward Lucas's room.

Movement in the dark hall drew my attention. I slid out of sight and pressed my back against the wall. A line of decrepit, zombie-like Shadow Lords entered the war room and shut the door behind them. I stepped lightly with slow, deliberate movements toward the door, gripping my full skirt to keep it from rustling as I walked. Kneeling on the ground, I looked through the brass key hole.

The rebel Shadow Lords and Shadow Spirits bowed to Lucas. He smiled and motioned for them to arise. Did Lucas understand what they were? Didn't he see they were rebels? Dark clouds formed around my fiancé. Lucas snatched one of the Shadow Lords by the tunic and lifted him into the air with one hand.

I covered my mouth. What was Lucas doing?

"Your Shadow Wolves couldn't take care of one mortal Watcher? Was the scent of venom not strong enough for your mangy dogs?" Lucas flicked his wrist and sent the Shadow Lord hurtling across the room. "I want her dead. She's not powerful enough right now. After she dies, I'm sure she will return as an Immortal for her precious Lucas. Then we will make her an Immortal queen."

"Master," one of the Shadow Lords addressed Lucas, "what about King Edward? Are we going to kill him and steal his body?"

Lucas shook his head. "The king is an easy puppet to control. I won't have anyone but me using such an influential human's body, and I won't give up this one yet." He pointed to his chest. "This human identity is too powerful a lure for the Lady of Neviah."

I covered my mouth to keep from screaming. It couldn't be true. There was only one way the rebel could have Lucas's image—he was Lucas's murderer. A dark reality crashed over me. The fire of revenge burned in my soul. I clenched my teeth and tears squeezed through my eyes.

I was such an imbecile. How could I let this happen? The pieces to this puzzle sorted out in my mind. Since Lucas had returned, he never came into the sunlight and his hands were always cold. He even snared me into an agreement of marriage. How could I be so foolish and blind?

The rebel in Lucas's body held up my ruby necklace. "Now that I have this, Lucas's mortal body won't decay until long after Auriella accepts me as her husband." The rebel curled his lips into a devilish smile. "Auriella will make a powerful queen and be the mother of a new Shadow empire. If she refuses, then . . ." He paused and laughed darkly. "She will not refuse me. I have her heart trapped in more ways than one."

A crippled woman hobbled from the crowd of rebels who surrounded Lucas.

"Hazella?" I gasped and my hands shook. This just kept getting worse.

Erebus took note of the old witch at his side. "You will be rewarded for helping to lead us to Auriella."

Hazella cackled and rubbed her hands together.

"Though you were born a Watcher, you have proven your loyalty to the Shadow Legion. What reward would you ask?" Lucas asked. He held up a leather bag and shook it. The unmistakable sound of coins clanking together resonated from inside.

"I be wantin' a greater reward than that gold," Hazella begged. "I be just as Neviahan as Auriella. Please take me ta be yer immortal Shadow Queen."

"You?" Lucas sneered. "But you are old, mortal, and barren. How can you be the mother of my damned offspring? I need a queen of power."

"I be a queen of power!" Hazella screamed and pointed at the ruby necklace Lucas wore. "Give me that there necklace and I be just as powerful as that wretched fire Watcher. Curse Auriella! Curse her and her Lifelight!"

Lucas fingered the necklace around his neck. "No," he said. "I will not give any of my power away. But if your desire is to be a Shadow Queen, there is another way."

"Anything." Hazella lowered her head worshipfully. "I be doing anything ta be immortal."

Erebus sneered. "I will strip you of this disgusting human image until you can find another. You must murder a human without damaging the body. Once she is dead, your dark spirit can become the host. Once that body grows old, you may abandon it and find another human body to take. In this way, you will have the immortality you crave."

"Yes!" Hazella crowed. "Yes, rid me of this body so I be findin' another."

Lucas stretched out his hand. Obsidian mist shot from his fingers, enveloping the old witch. Blood oozed from her mouth, eyes, and ears. She shrieked as her body convulsed. Her hands strained in pain. Her white hair fell to the floor like dead straw. Hazella's colorless eyes whirled in agony before they dropped from the sockets and bounced along the ground. Her flesh and muscles fell off her bones like a moth-eaten cloak. All that remained was her writhing skeletal frame. The jaw bone hung open, still screaming.

Despite my dislike for the witch, my stomach turned watching Hazella suffer a hellish torture. Peaceful death refused to act out mercy.

Finally Hazella's bones crumbed into ash and her dark spirit was all that remained. A sinister laugh replaced her shrieking scream.

"Go now and find your new human body," Erebus instructed Hazella's dark spirit.

I fell back from the door and scrambled to my feet. My heart pounded. I moved clumsily as I fought to keep my balance on stiff legs and raced down the hallways back to my room. Hopefully Azrael, Korban, and Orion were already there waiting for me. I didn't want to be alone after what I had just seen.

I threw open my door and looked around the dark room.

"They will be back any moment," I told myself. I tried to compose my emotions and still my trembling body so I could report my discovery without breaking down into tears.

I wrapped my arms around my waist and stumbled to the balcony doors. The man I promised my hand to was not the boy I'd known in my childhood—he was Lucas's murderer. I couldn't believe I hadn't seen all the signs. I was so happy Lucas had returned that I was blind to what he really was.

I opened the balcony doors and stepped outside. The dark clouds of Erebus's storm shrouded all light. All of this was my fault. I should have never gone to Scotland. For all I knew, it was actually Erebus who fed lies to the king until he ordered me to go. Maybe they were just trying to get me out of the way so Erebus's army could invade London.

I pulled at my hair. How could I have been so foolish to turn my Watcher duty over to the Shadow King himself just because he looked like Lucas? I willingly gave Erebus my ruby necklace that healed him in battle. I gripped the railing and doubled over as queasiness hit me. This had to be the most idiotic thing a Watcher had ever done.

I retreated back inside, grasped the cold brass handles of the balcony doors, and pulled them shut. There had to be something I could do to amend my mistakes. I turned around and almost touched noses with the beast I hated most in the world.

Erebus smiled slyly at me with Lucas's lips.

I pressed my back against the balcony doors and stared into his face. My hand trembled as I gripped the handle of the sword at my waist. I imagined running my sword through his body and braced myself to do it.

He yanked my sword from the scabbard and tossed it across the room.

I tried not to act surprised or afraid. He leaned against the doors with one hand on either side of me and pressed closer. His icy breath washed over my ear.

"You have been crying. What is wrong, my love?" He slid his bitter cold arms around me. I stiffened at the lack of human warmth in his touch. I searched his black eyes that were once cornflower blue. I wanted desperately for him to be Lucas. "We are going to have the wedding ceremony tomorrow," he said. "You will be my queen and fight by my side as we always dreamed."

I swallowed the hard lump in my throat. I'd rather die than aid the Shadow Legion in destroying the human race.

The Shadow King took my hand and kissed it. He had done the same thing many times, but this time I shivered from the icy touch as his lips brushed across my skin. "My love, I got a report that there are three rebels in the castle. I'm going to stay with you tonight to protect you. Trust me. Let me watch you sleep tonight, my future queen." He leaned in to kiss my neck.

I pushed him away with strained hands. "It is not proper."

He gripped my hands and pressed them against his chest. "I do not care about propriety."

I tried to pull away while keeping my voice overly sweet. "I am finishing my dress tonight, and it is not proper for you to see it before our wedding."

"I see," Erebus said with a smile. "If you will kiss me before I go, I will be satisfied until the morning."

I tightened my fists and fought to hold my composure. I didn't want to kiss him—I wanted to kill him. The Shadow King frowned and realized, "You don't know how to sew." His eyes flashed with smoldering brimstone.

My breath quickened as I stared into Erebus's eyes, still searching for any sign of the man I loved. "What have you done to Lucas?" I tried to pull away.

"Lucas is dead. I not only took his body, but all his memories of you." He grinned, his teeth now pointed and dagger-like. "Do you know who I am, my lady?"

My voice broke. I couldn't get in the breath to speak.

"I am Erebus, Shadow King of the Damned." He leaned closer, hovering over me. "I'm not as evil as the Neviahan king thinks I am. I'm actually quite good and I'm offering you everything you've ever wanted and a throne by my side. I offer you power, fame, wealth, and

. . . my passion." His harsh whisper echoed as if he shouted it. "Don't you dare refuse me."

My mouth hung open in awe at his bold, but empty offer. Did he really think I would actually consider joining him when it was my destiny to destroy him? I stared at the sapphire ring burning on my hand. "I . . . I need some time to think about this," I stalled, hoping the three Immortals would walk in the door any moment and save me.

Erebus pulled away. "I will have your answer tomorrow morning. If you fight against me, more will die, including your new Watcher friends." His words bit into me like the fangs of a venomous snake. Erebus snatched one of my red locks and twisted it around his finger before letting it fall onto my chest. He smiled, and embers smoldered in his eyes before he turned and left.

Once the door was shut and I was alone, I braced myself against the vanity. My rainbow ring glinted from the tabletop. I couldn't believe I ever took it off. The Fairy Queen gave it to me when I first discovered I was a Neviahan. She told me it should always remind me that just like the rainbow, I was from the heavens. The rainbow ring slid easily back onto my hand, right where it belonged.

Bad things happen to everyone. I cannot control all the horrible things that happen in my life, but I can control whether my trials make me weaker or make me stronger.

I picked up my fallen sword. Erebus and the Shadow Legion should be terrified of me. They had done me so much wrong, but instead of weakening me, the Legion drove me to find the strength and determination of an entire army.

I would show them I remembered who I was. Flames shot from my hands and enveloped my sword.

Chapter Sixteen

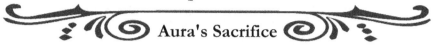 Aura's Sacrifice

Orion and Korban burst into my room and barricaded themselves against the door.

"Thirty-three Shadow Lords and two Shadow Wolves," Korban said with a wide grin. Shadow blood covered their battle kilts and bare chests like proud war paint. "That's a new record for us."

"Lucas is Erebus," I sputtered and took a deep breath. "He was pretending to be Lucas all along." I lowered my head. "I was deceived."

"We were all deceived," Korban said while holding the door shut with Orion.

I hoped part of Lucas was still alive.

"What color were his eyes?" Orion asked.

"Black," I said. "Very black."

"Then Lucas is dead," Orion confirmed my fear.

"Erebus doesn't fight fair," Korban said. His eyes flashed to the doors as the sound of footsteps grew louder. "Don't let regret distract you from what we have to do now. They are coming."

I ran to the door and helped them brace it with my feeble mortal strength.

Orion eyed me up and down. "And you thought how we dressed for battle was inappropriate."

I glanced at my midnight black stowaway outfit. There wasn't anything wrong with what I wore for battling the Shadows. Black pants and high boots sheathed my legs. I had just finished lacing up the soft black leather corset when they came in. It was a different look for a woman, but perfect for a warrior like me who depended on agility and flexibility.

Korban let out an impressed whistle. He had to be mocking me.

"Really?" I said and lowered my head to hide the sudden flush to my face. "You don't expect me to go after Erebus in a ball gown, do you?"

The footsteps grew louder. "'Tis Azrael. Let him in," Orion said. We scrambled out of the way and Orion momentarily opened the door for him.

Azrael slid into the door frame and ricocheted ungracefully into the room. It was the first time I'd seen him do something clumsy. Baby bounded in behind him. "I saw at least a hundred more in the main hall." Azrael froze when he saw me dressed for battle. "Whoa!" His face relaxed, and he dropped his hard stance and grinned like a fool suddenly hit by Cupid's arrow.

I kept a straight face. "I know, it's not very ladylike, but you better get used to it if we are going to be fighting side by side for the rest of my time on Earth."

He brushed back his hair with one hand, but didn't stop smiling. "It might be a little distracting, but I'd be more than happy with that."

More footsteps pounded from the hallway. Azrael spun around and peered out the doors. "Blast! They're coming."

"How many?" Korban asked.

"600, at least," Azrael answered.

"Can we take on 600 strong?" I asked.

Korban narrowed his eyes. "Maybe, but not without risking Aura."

Azrael glanced at me. "Can we outrun them if I carry Aura?"

Korban shook his head. "Do you know what that kind of speed would do to a mortal?"

I suddenly felt like the liability I didn't want to be. It was best they run away without me and save themselves. I wasn't trying to be a martyr—I just didn't want Erebus to drink their blood and steal the power of four Neviahans instead of one.

The lamplight from the balcony reflected in Azrael's silver eyes. "Come with me. I've got an idea."

Korban, Baby, Orion, and I followed Azrael to the balcony. Azrael peered over the edge at the vines climbing up the castle wall. "Orion, can you—"

"Already on it." Orion lifted his hands into the air. A sound like rustling leaves resonated through the courtyard below and grew louder. I looked over the edge of the balcony. The vines twisted and thickened by the second as they reached toward us.

The Legion pounded on the doors from behind. I whirled around and gripped the edge of the railing. The wood of the doors bowed as the Shadow Lords and Shadow Wolves made siege on my bedroom chamber. "They're breaking through." Wood shattered as the enemy flooded the room.

Azrael slammed the balcony doors shut. Korban and I helped Azrael brace them. My boots slid against the stone as I pressed my back against the doors with all my might.

"Ready," Orion said. "One at a time."

"Go, Aura!" Azrael shouted. I left the doors which added more weight for the others to hold. I could hear the Shadow Wolves on the other side, snarling and scratching at the doors. I gripped the vines and slid down two stories to the courtyard below. My feet hit the bottom with more shock than I intended, and my legs tingled from the blow.

Korban climbed down next, followed by Orion with Baby draped over his shoulders.

I furrowed my brow. "Azrael is holding the doors alone?" I asked Korban. He didn't say anything. I shook my head and repressed the horrible image of him being stabbed in the heart and having his immortality destroyed.

Once Orion hit the ground and set Baby down, Korban called, "Now, Azrael!"

Azrael didn't appear over the balcony. I gripped my sword tighter and counted the seconds he didn't answer.

"Azrael!" I yelled.

No reply.

Korban shifted his weight.

Baby paced and looked at the balcony.

"I'm going after him," I said.

Korban gripped my arm. "Wait."

Azrael's silhouette sprang from the balcony and stretched spread eagle in the air. His body whirled around. He snatched the vines and swung wide like a pendulum.

The Shadow Lords hacked the vines with their swords and tossed daggers at him.

The vine snapped. Azrael freefell, twisting his body like a cat, before landing lightly on his feet. Obviously feline grace was another trait he inherited when Baby became his animal companion. Azrael stalked toward me with a proud grin. "Did I give you a fright, my lady?"

I narrowed my eyes. "You are too reckless, Azrael." I wanted to slap him and kissed him at the same time.

Azrael's eyes opened wide behind his dark mask. A smile flared across his immortal face.

I drew my sword as Shadow Lords and Shadow Wolves flooded the courtyard from the arched hallways.

Arrows sprang from bent bows and shot toward us like lethal hail. Azrael raised his hand. A gust of wind caught the arrows and suspended them in flight. He flicked his wrist and the arrows turned and rained down on the advancing Legionnaires.

"Brilliant!" I complimented.

The advancing army crashed against Korban. Metal sang as his blades sliced through the rebel's line. I encircled myself in a protective ring of fire. Streams of flames burst from my fingertips and out the end of my sword. I shot a ball of fire at the pack of wolves, but it didn't stop them. They seemed to feel no pain even as their fur and flesh burned off their bodies. Orion's axe pounded down on a wolf. The beast's head rolled toward the base of the castle, its venomous jaw still snapping wildly.

"Keep firing!" Orion shouted at me. "I've got your back!"

I nodded and summoned all the energy in my body. Steady streams of inferno poured from my hands.

Baby lunged for a Shadow Wolf. The usually tender-eyed feline went wild with rage, teeth and claws sinking into the wolf, shredding the dark flesh and fur from the wolf's body.

Shadow Lords in stolen human bodies and wispy black Spirits of Shadow surrounded us.

The ground trembled.

"Erebus," Azrael growled.

The Spirits of Shadow and Shadow Lords cheered as their master approached. Erebus's steps hit the earth like an executioner's drum. The Shadow King laughed and pointed at me. "There you are, my Neviahan pet."

"Lucas?" Azrael gasped. He hadn't been there when I told Orion and Korban about Erebus. Azrael glanced back at me. I looked away, still ashamed I had been deceived.

Brimstone flared in Erebus's eyes and the ground trembled as he roared. Erebus leaned forward and eyed me with hunger.

I positioned my sword between myself and the dark creature in Lucas's body.

He whipped his hand through the air and pulled the sword from my grasp without even touching it.

Azrael raced toward me. With a single glance, Erebus tossed Azrael across the courtyard into Baby. They both hit the castle wall and slid to the ground. Azrael stood and braced himself as rebels surrounded him. Baby hissed with all the rage of a wild cat.

Erebus raised his hand and pointed at me. Nothing happened. He narrowed his eyes and flicked his wrist like a whip. Whatever spell he was trying to cast didn't work on me. He clenched his teeth and pointed at the balcony above. The stones broke away from the main castle and crumbled over my head.

"Look out!" Korban yelled.

I held my hands up. A flaming shield sprang from my flesh and covered my body. The rubble crashed over me.

My fingers and toes felt like ice as the last of my energy burned. My fire shield extinguished and rubble fell down on me.

I shook my head, trying to repel the pain of the attack. My whole body ached as I fought to catch my breath under the pile of rocks.

Blood tricked down my forehead like sweat. I couldn't let Erebus have my blood and steal my powers. Whatever happened, I couldn't let him win this battle.

Wind rushed between the cracks around me and soaked into my skin. "Azrael," I whispered. His energy fed me. "Don't touch my blood," I warned.

Hot flames erupted from my body, bursting the boulders around me. I pushed myself up from the debris. My fingers sank into the burning embers. Smoldering shards of wood rolled down my hair into my face. The fire blazed at my feet, healing the gashes along my skin.

I stood regally, opening my palms and absorbing the heat. The fire extinguished and the courtyard went black like the shrouded night. The steady thump of my own heartbeat pounded in the pitch darkness as I inhaled.

When I exhaled a blinding light burst from my body. Hot flames blazed off my shoulders and swirled wildly like ribbons of light. The inferno raised high above my head and danced around my frame. The rebels cowered and backed away from the heat.

Azrael smirked at Erebus. "You're in trouble now. You shouldn't have made her mad."

Erebus froze and stared at me with wide eyes.

I harnessed the energy and formed it into a glowing sphere of light. The intense orb rotated in my hands, growing in size and velocity. I thrust the hot light into the rebel army. They burst into ash as the explosion struck them. My hair swirled around my face like living wind and fire as I prepared to attack again.

Azrael, Orion, Korban, and Baby took defensive positions and blocked the rebels approaching from behind. Mounds of ash littered the ground around us.

Erebus pointed at me and screamed, "Stop her! Stop her!"

More Spirits of Shadow emerged from the ground and floated toward us.

My powers quickly drained and my arms and legs went stiff and cold as ice. I needed more sunlight. My knees hit the ground and the fire around me dimmed.

"Aura?" Azrael shouted.

"'Tis her energy," Orion said.

"Fall back!" Korban commanded.

I wasn't going to stop fighting. I had to avenge Lucas. "No!" I would fight with or without my powers. I searched for my sword.

"Fall back!" Korban said again.

I yanked the dagger from my boot. "I will not be moved!"

Azrael dashed toward me, grabbed my hips, and tossed me over his shoulder like a sack of potatoes.

"You can't do this, Azrael!" I complained. "The battle is not over. Put me down this instant or I will—"

"Or what?" Azrael challenged. "You'll use your powers against me and blow up the whole castle? You don't have much left after that dramatic fire show." Azrael laughed at me, which only made me angrier. He raced toward the stables with me still over his shoulder. "This fight 'tis over. We will return with reinforcements."

I ground my teeth together and pounded on his back. His shoulder blades were as hard as marble. "I have to fight Erebus," I demanded. Stone walls and torches streamed past us. "Erebus has my ruby necklace."

"I'll buy you a new one," Azrael promised.

He and the other Neviahans raced out the corridor to the stables. He set me on my feet, but stood like a barricade between me and the door so I couldn't return to the fight.

"You don't understand. It's a necklace that can heal," I explained. "I have to get it back or we won't be able to ever defeat Erebus."

Orion and Korban mounted their horses.

Korban shook his head at me. "If he steals the power of Starfire, then it will be impossible to defeat him."

Azrael tossed a saddle onto his horse with one hand while holding my wrist so I couldn't run back to the courtyard.

He was about to saddle my horse, but Korban stopped him. "We've got to hurry," he said. "Aura's horse is still healing and will be too slow."

Azrael lifted me onto his horse and leapt up behind me. His arms locked around me like immortal steel.

"No!" I shouted. If I left now, they would never let me return for my revenge. All I could see was the color red. I wanted revenge.

Azrael gripped the reins. "Yah!" he bellowed. The horse took off at a fast gallop from the stables through the streets of London.

I sat rigid in Azrael's arms, helpless against his strength, but still angry at him.

"I'm sorry," he whispered in my ear.

I shrugged and looked away. The cold night air whipped the hot tears from my face. The horses' hooves echoed off the London Bridge as we galloped full speed toward the city boundaries.

The horse reared up in surprise and slid to a halt. Azrael, Orion, and Korban struggled to gain control over the frightened animals. Obsidian mist enveloped us in a tsunami of darkness. Not even the light of the moon penetrated the blanket of icy gloom.

"Did you think you could get away that easily?" Erebus seethed as he stepped through the darkness. Shadow Wolves and Shadow Lords surrounded us on all sides. Hungry Spirits of Shadow floated overhead.

Azrael drew his sword and held it in the air. "We won't surrender without a fight."

Erebus laughed. "Do you know how powerful I could be if I drank the blood of four more Neviahans?"

The Shadow Wolves stalked closer. The hair on my arms stood as the reality of death became inevitable. This battle was over. The four of us couldn't defeat Erebus and his army. If Azrael and I used Starfire there was no way Korban, Orion, and Baby would survive.

Erebus didn't know that Azrael was my key or he would have already killed us and taken the power of Starfire.

"Wait," I said. "You don't want them." If there was going to be any blood drinking I had to find a way to save Azrael to protect the power of Starfire.

Erebus laced his spider-like hands together. His pupils narrowed to a slit as he focused on me. "Why not?" he asked coolly.

"What do you want more? The power of four Watchers or a Shadow Queen?" I asked.

Erebus dropped his hands to his sides. "Are you saying you will come with me willingly back to the castle?"

"If you let them go," I agreed.

Azrael's hand covered my mouth. His lips pressed against my ear. "You don't know what you're doing. If he takes you as queen, you will give birth to an army we could never defeat. It is best we die fighting him now. Use Starfire and blow the whole of London up."

Two Shadow Lords gripped Azrael, yanked him from the horse, and slammed him against the road. They held a dagger over his heart—the one place where, if struck, could kill an Immortal.

"No." I jumped from the horse. A Shadow Lord gripped me from behind and locked my shoulders in place.

Orion and Korban were on their feet, ready to fight.

"Stop, Erebus, stop them!" I tried to pull away.

Erebus held up his hand, and the Shadow Lords removed the dagger.

I took a deep breath and gazed into Azrael's beautiful eyes behind his cursed mask. This was the only way I could save him, all of London, and protect Starfire.

Erebus strode toward me. His eyes narrowed as if searching my soul.

"Please don't hurt them," I begged. "Let them go and I will stay."

"No!" Azrael roared. "We do not fear them that kill the body, but, Aura, don't let him kill your soul!"

I swallowed hard and looked at Azrael for the last time.

Erebus's fingers curled like claws around my face and forced me to look at him. "Come with me to the castle and I will do no harm to your friends."

I glanced down at the ruby necklace around his neck and nodded. Erebus's cold hands pressed against my ribs and followed the contours of my waist down to my hips. "You finally made the right decision." He whipped the edge of his cloak through the air and tossed it over us. The world went dark as the Shadow King and I disappeared into a shroud of mist.

Chapter Seventeen

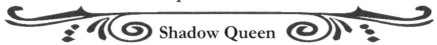 Shadow Queen

Erebus clenched the back of my neck and shoved me into my room. "Prepare yourself for our wedding. I will be waiting in the king's chambers for you." He commanded several Shadow Lords to stand watch outside so I couldn't escape.

As soon as he slammed the door, I searched the room for any weapon I could use to exact my revenge. I found a dagger and a dull sword. They would have to do. I couldn't live with myself if I didn't eliminate the Shadow King. He murdered my fiancé and tricked me into loving him.

Once I killed Erebus I doubt I would be able to get past the army of Legionnaires or the pack of wolves waiting outside—this was a suicide mission. I dropped my shoulders. At least the Legion wouldn't get the power of Starfire without Azrael's blood too.

My knee-high leather boots clicked on the stone tile as I marched to the balcony doors and flung them open. The cold night air washed the scent of death and bonfires over me. My tailored black leather armor reflected the silver moonlight breaking through

Erebus's storm. The city glittered below like a sea of stars and the river Thames laced through London like a black snake.

I grabbed onto the thick ivy vines growing like a sheet along the side of the castle and crept up the wall. Pulling myself onto the king's balcony, I crouched low like a black jungle cat. The curtains billowed in the wind, revealing the Shadow King pacing the room with his hands balled into fists at his sides. I watched and waited for the right moment to attack.

Erebus glanced into the hallway and shouted, "What's taking her so long?" He slammed the door shut and turned to the room.

I whipped back my dagger and flung it between the curtains. The blade skimmed across Erebus's neck and stuck into the bedpost. Erebus held his hand over his neck as black, tar-like blood oozed from the wound. The wound closed up as his flesh mended together. I glared at the ruby necklace hanging over his chest. If I was going to have any chance of winning this fight, I had to get my necklace back.

I bounded through the doors, jump-kicked, and slammed the heel of my boot into his face.

His head snapped back as he fell to the floor, momentarily stunned. I whirled to the door and slipped the lock in place before his guards could interfere.

Erebus braced himself against the bed and rose to his feet. "Resister!" he hissed, sounding more like a snake than a human.

I unsheathed the sword at my side. My long hair flamed around my angry face. "You have something of mine." I pointed to the necklace he wore. "And I have something of yours." I flicked my sapphire engagement ring at him.

Erebus snatched the ring in his hand and tightened his fist. Glittering gem dust seeped between his fingers and showered onto the ground. "Fool!"

I positioned my sword between us. "Are you afraid to fight me without the necklace to protect you?"

Erebus tore the ruby necklace from his neck and dropped it onto the bed. "I have the powers of a dozen Neviahans, and your precious blood will be mine as well." His eyes glistened with terror and envy. Though his voice shook with fear, he laughed. "And I have you here, all alone, to myself. The best part is, you are still a fragile mortal." He laughed again, sounding more confident. "Where are your kingdom's brave warriors? If the King of Neviah still cared for you, he would send armies to your aid." Erebus wrapped his fingers around Lucas's sword, and his eyes flashed with fury. The Shadow King lunged for me with the blade extended.

I blocked his assault and thrust the tip of my sword into his shoulder. Glistening obsidian blood oozed from Lucas's body. Erebus didn't react to the pain.

"Lucas taught you well. I had all his memories of you come to me as I drained the life out of him," he taunted.

I pulled my weapon from his body and stepped back, battling the emotions raging inside me.

"Stand down, Auriella," Erebus said, ignoring the new wound. "You have no chance of winning this fight." He whipped his blade toward me.

I raised my sword with one hand and blocked the force of his massive blow. "I will not stand down!" Strength rushed through my veins as if I were standing in the sun.

His expression hardened. "No Earthling has ever stood their ground against me and lived."

My lips lifted in an impish smile. "I'm not from Earth." The hair on my arms stood and chills raced up my body as warmth filled my heart. Flames sprang from my hands and enveloped me like armor. Sparkling fire danced off my sword, creating a vortex of heat as I whirled the weapon and slammed the Shadow King against the wall.

Erebus's look of shock melted as he taunted, "Go ahead, destroy Lucas's body."

I hesitated for a split second.

Erebus took the opening to strike. Sparks sprayed off my hot blade. He struck again, knocking the sword from my hand. Lucas's sword sliced deep into my palm.

I screamed in pain and clenched my teeth together. Blood gushed out my hand and dripped down my fingers into a puddle on the stone floor. I held my hand close to my body to stop the blood from rushing out.

Healing fire sprang from my hands and the pain subsided. I opened my palm and examined the pink scar marking my skin.

Erebus twisted his lips into a grin and motioned toward the necklace on the bed. "Now why would someone who can heal themselves carry a necklace like this?" He reached out with inhuman speed and gripped my wrists. My fingers throbbed under the crushing pressure of his strength. "Is it because you can't heal broken bones?"

Snap!

I tensed and bit my lip, refusing to give him the pleasure of hearing me scream in pain.

Erebus dropped me onto the floor. I held both my broken arms to my chest.

He bent down and whispered into my ear. "Or are you hoping that one day the necklace will heal your heart?"

I glanced at the Shadow King wearing and controlling Lucas's body like a glove. I had experienced too much loss, betrayal, and abandonment in this life to ever heal.

Erebus snatched me from the floor and held my back to his chest. His arms locked around me in a suffocating vice. "I'm giving you this last chance to live." Erebus placed the necklace around my neck and connected the clasp. My arms filled with heat as the healing power of the necklace mended my bones. "I have the power to make all your pain go away." He unclasped the necklace and held it in front of my face. "If you refuse, your powers will still aid us. All it takes is for you to be dead." He pulled a dagger from the sleeve of his shirt and inhaled greedily. "I have no doubt your blood will be the sweetest I have ever tasted."

I braced myself as the cold metal touched my neck.

His breath penetrated my skin like icy daggers as he spoke. "This is your last chance. Join with us and live."

I swallowed the lump in my throat and forced my unyielding answer. "Never!"

The doors slammed against the walls. The wood shattered into splinters. A torrent of wind whipped my hair around my face like a wild fire. Several Shadow Lords hit the ground. Black blood oozed from their lifeless bodies. Azrael stepped into the room and held out his Scottish broad-sword. Shadow blood-stained his tunic and glistened off his boots.

"Azrael?" I gasped. Why would that idiot come back? Now we were both going to die, and Erebus would have the power of Starfire.

"How romantic," Erebus seethed. "The fourth son of the Neviahan king has come to rescue his lady. Still wearing your cursed mask, I see—brother."

"Azrael, run!" I screamed.

A surge of wind whirled debris through the room. Azrael advanced.

Erebus's blade bit into my neck.

I gasped as my warm blood streamed down my cold skin.

Azrael halted.

"You aren't my brother anymore," Azrael said. "Not since you chose to rebel against father and abandon our kingdom."

Erebus cast me aside and pointed the dagger at Azrael. "Father cursed us! He took away our powers, and I am only taking back what is mine by drinking Watcher blood." Erebus stepped forward. I slid against the wall and held my hand to the wound on my neck. "Earth is ours now," Erebus shouted. "No one is going to drive me out of my kingdom I'm creating on Earth." Saliva flew from his lips as he spoke. "It's you who are invading our kingdom on Earth with your celestial light."

Azrael glanced at me and looked at the blood on the floor from when my hand was split open. "What about the humans?" Azrael asked. "Earth is their home."

Erebus took a step toward Azrael. "Humans are too much like you Watchers. They need to be destroyed while they are still weak." He tilted his head back and laughed. "It was too easy to figure out your weakness, Prince Azrael." He turned from Azrael and pointed at me.

"You're right, Aura is my weakness." A smile escaped Azrael's lips. "But she is also my strength." Azrael jolted forward and shot a ball of fire into my blood on the floor.

I ducked my head and covered my ears. The explosion seemed to shake every bone in my body. The fire-ball blazed with heat and slammed me against the wall. Blue and white flames tore through the room, disintegrating everything in its path. The stones smoldered and cracked from the heat. My ears rang inside my buzzing skull.

Azrael gripped my hand and pulled me into his arms. "We've got to go!" My head whirled from the force of the explosion. Azrael carried me through the inferno to the remains of the balcony. Waves of heat swirled around us in suffocating pressure as it consumed the oxygen.

"Azrael," I gasped out his name. Why did he take us to the balcony? The castle tower was collapsing. The stones under his feet cracked and the tower shook. I looked over the balcony railing to the stone courtyard three levels down.

"You can thank me later," he said, then added, "If we live." He wrapped one arm around the small of my back. "Hang on."

I leaned into his chest and ducked my head. There was no way we could survive this fall. Azrael pressed me close to him. He leaped into the sky away from the crumbling tower.

The ground seemed to be rising and we plummeted toward the earth. I gripped Azrael tighter and imagined my whole body broken, like my arms had been before the necklace healed me. Cold air streamed past us, whipping our hair and clothes against our bodies.

"Brace yourself." Azrael rolled onto his back to act as a buffer between me and the cobblestone courtyard. I buried my face into his chest. The wind pushed up against us in a swirling vortex, slowing our speed before we smacked against the ground. The stones under Azrael's body cracked.

I lifted my head and pushed myself off his motionless body.

"Azrael!" I screamed. "Say something." A fall like that, even with a little wind resistance, should have put him in survival sleep.

Azrael moaned.

I brushed his hair back and stroked his face.

Azrael sat up, put his hand to the back of his head, and smiled. "I told you I would steal you away from him."

"Azrael." I tried not to laugh. "That fall rattled your brain."

Clanking chain mail and clicking boots on stone echoed from the castle.

"Time to go." Azrael jumped to his feet and snatched my hand. We raced from the courtyard to the stables.

"Do you think my horse will make it?" I asked, wondering about her healing legs.

"We have no choice," Azrael answered.

Azrael flung open the stable doors. A Shadow Lord held my horse by the reins and fired a crossbow.

Azrael caught the arrow in mid-flight and flung it into the Shadow Lord's neck. Another rebel dropped from the rafters behind Azrael. I hurled my dagger and stuck the Shadow Lord in the eye socket. Azrael spun around as the rebel fell to the ground.

Azrael whistled. "Impressive."

I curtsied like a lady. "Not as impressive as you catching arrows in mid-flight."

Azrael's eyes danced with joy behind his mask. "It helps when you can control the wind." He boosted me up onto my horse, mounted behind me, and grabbed the reins.

"'Tis nice that I don't have to hold you down this time," he teased. Azrael flexed his arms around me. We took off at a fast gallop through the back streets of London to avoid the Legion. Azrael and I burst through the gates leading out of the city and rode into the dark forest. "Keep your sights straight ahead of you," Azrael warned. "Do not look back."

Chapter Eighteen

Warrior's Death

Shame and guilt ate at my heart like acid. I blinked several times to hold back my tears. It was my duty to protect London from the Shadow Legion, and now it was overrun. Humans would start dying at a rapid rate from whatever plague Erebus had in store for them. It was all because of me. My body quivered from more than just the cold north wind and assailing storm.

"Are you well?" Azrael asked, his voice pulling me back to the present.

My mind couldn't erase the events from last night. "I feel like a lady-in-waiting with nothing to wait for, and a knight for a kingdom that has fallen." I kept my eyes straight ahead of me and avoided eye contact with Azrael so I wouldn't break down into tears.

Azrael touched my hand. I ignored the white sparks skittering up my arm. The Starfire energy rushed faster than lightning through every vein in my body, then back down my arm into Azrael's hand.

"'Tis over now," he whispered. "Everything will be fine once we reach the sanctuary."

I nodded, but doubted. There was still so much work to do. How were we going to take back London?

We rounded the bend in the road and met up with Korban and Orion waiting with Baby and Azrael's horse. Recognition flickered in their eyes and they relaxed when they saw us.

Orion dropped his shoulders and let out a gust of air as if he had been holding his breath. "'Tis you."

Baby charged toward us, startling the horse.

"Whoa," Azrael called. Baby reluctantly took a few steps back and waited for Azrael to dismount.

Azrael held my hand and helped me from my horse. My body was so exhausted I collapsed into his arms. Normally, I would have pulled away, but I just stood there, resting against his chest as my tears soaked the front of his shirt. "Please forgive me," I whispered. "I almost married someone I wasn't in love with." I opened my mouth to say "I really love you," but couldn't press out the words past the emotion.

Azrael gently crushed me against his chest and kissed the top of my head. "You only did what you thought was best. It was noble of you to willingly sacrifice yourself to save human lives and protect Starfire. You put the happiness of others above your own, and I cannot blame you for that."

It only made me more emotional that he was so forgiving.

Azrael stroked my hair. "We have to go through hell to get to heaven." He gazed into my eyes as if diving into my soul. "I have my heaven, right here in my arms."

I caught my breath and bravely allowed myself to get lost in the depths of his beauty and benevolence. I reached up and traced the cursed mask around his eyes. I savored the passionate and tender feelings orbiting my heart. "There's something I want to say to you." I held my breath and prepared to break his curse by confessing my love for him.

"Azrael, Aura!" Korban shouted. "We've got to leave now."

Azrael's gaze shot to the billowing obsidian clouds of vengeance blanketing the sky and forbidding morning to ever come.

Baby's fur stood like the needles of a pine tree. He watched the darkening woods with wary eyes, and jumped at the slightest movement.

"We are going to split into two groups," Korban said. "It will be harder for the Shadow Wolves to track us if we head in opposite directions. In the morning, we will loop around and meet at Swansea."

Red lightning whipped across the sky. Instead of thunder, the heavens echoed with a screech like a banshee. Icy pellets of rain hit my skin. I swallowed hard. The sheer terror of being hunted like prey hit me. Chills ran down my spine as if the Shadow Wolf's hot breath already washed over me.

Dark clouds of mist crashed through the forest like the waves of an ocean storm and shrouded us in darkness.

The horses stomped at the ground. I blinked, forcing my eyes to adjust quickly to the deepening darkness.

"Blast!" Korban cursed. "We don't have much of a head start." The rain drizzled into puddles forming along the dirt road. "I will ride east with Orion." Korban pointed at Azrael and instructed, "You ride west with Aura. Don't let anything happen to her, or the High Druid of Fire will have your head."

"I'm not worried about my head." Azrael pulled me under his arm. "It's my heart I'm worried about. I won't lose her."

Lightning flashed and shrieking thunder echoed across the dark rolling hills. Sheets of rain fell in waves and pounded against the muddy road. Orion was the only one wearing a cloak. He removed it and handed it to Azrael. Azrael draped the warm cloak around me and connected the clasp. "Are you ready, Aura?" he asked.

I nodded. Whether I was ready or not, we had to go.

"The storm will wash our scent away," Azrael assured me. "By the time the Shadow Wolves pick up our trail, we will be miles away from England and halfway to the sanctuary."

Korban tightened his jaw. He bounded onto his horse, yanked on the reins, and turned east.

Orion put his massive hand on Azrael's shoulder. "Ride hard, my friend."

Azrael returned the gesture with his strong grip. "Godspeed, my brother in arms."

Orion mounted and turned east with Korban. Their horses took off at a sprint and the two disappeared into the shrouded forest. I couldn't help but wonder if this was the last time I would see them. They didn't say it, but I knew Korban and Orion took the more dangerous road. They were acting as decoys.

Azrael turned to me. He kept his voice low and calm despite the urgent circumstances. "I will ride on your right and Baby will run on your left. We are your shields. No matter what happens, stay between us."

I nodded. Azrael lifted me onto my horse as if I were weightless. My hands gripped the slick, wet reins until my knuckles turned white and pulsed for release. I was a warrior. I had to keep fighting. I had to stay strong. I had to stay focused. I looked at the dark road ahead of me. I wasn't going to let fear conquer me. I narrowed my eyes with determination and kicked my horse's ribs.

The thundering hooves hit the ground and sprayed dark pools of mud into the air. Baby and Azrael kept my pace. The cold wind whistled past me and whipped the rain from my warm cheeks.

Lightning flashed overhead, illuminating the stormy indigo clouds dominating the sky. I kept my horse steady. The skies lit up again with electric fury. I memorized the road ahead and stayed the course when the world went black between flashes.

Hours passed and the rain died to a light shower, but we didn't let up on our speed.

I glanced to my left and met Azrael's silver eyes. With his ability to see through the darkness, he was not only my protector, but my guide as well. We rode hard until the moonlight broke through the clouds.

I had never seen such a bright night. The moon coated my skin with silver light and streaked across my hair making it shimmer. Every star seemed bigger and more glorious after escaping the Legion's shroud. I relaxed my arms and slowed my pace to a trot. Azrael and Baby followed my lead. Mud drenched Baby's silky white fur and caked his massive paws. He slunk forward along the trail, watching the woods dutifully.

I gripped my wet cloak tighter under my chin and whispered, "Thank you for coming back for me." They were the first words either of us had spoken in hours.

"Always." Azrael reached for my hand. White sparks flew between our fingers. I didn't pull away from his touch, but let my fingers intertwine with his. The embrace felt natural, peaceful, and instinctual. My heart didn't race like I thought it would, but instead I felt stronger, braver, and loved.

"Do you think Korban and Orion will be all right?" I asked.

Azrael laughed. "Those two can take on a whole pack of Shadow Wolves."

I pulled away from his captivating gaze and looked up at the North Star.

Azrael stared into the heavens with me. His energy combined with mine through our joined hands and he pointed at two bright lights in the sky. "Venus and Mars align tonight. The mythical goddess of love and god of war make peace."

I smiled and savored his warm velvety voice. A bright light streaked across the sky. I gasped. "A falling star. We should make a wish."

"You first," Azrael offered.

He was too good to me. I knew exactly what I wanted. "I wish for humans to have peace someday." I lowered my head. Because of me, their peace would be delayed. "I feel like I've ruined everything."

"You are a wonderful Watcher, and an extraordinary woman," Azrael assured. "All Watchers are given training for Earth combat before they leave the kingdom. The king wouldn't have sent you to Earth if you weren't ready to fight."

"I wish I could remember my training. Some of those moves might come in handy."

"'Tis all right if we make mistakes." Azrael thoughtfully added, "We never completed all our training in Neviah. We are supposed to finish our training here on Earth. We will be much stronger when we return home victorious."

I couldn't help but smile. He knew just what to say when I was emotionally beating myself up. "Do you think we knew how hard it would be on Earth?"

I could sense Azrael choosing his words carefully. "Do you regret hosting a human body?"

I took a deep breath and thought about my answer. "Well, I have learned a lot since I came to Earth." My memories seemed like a fluid dream I could swim through. I thought about all the humans I had ever loved. "No," I answered, then added, "I don't ever want to relive my past, but I'm glad I went through it. My experiences have made me who I am."

Azrael smiled like he had made his point.

"I can't imagine what you've been through in your long life," I said.

Azrael's eyes sparkled like the stars overhead. "I'm still learning to be a good Watcher myself."

"What are your earliest memories?" I prodded.

"My earliest memories on Earth?" Azrael stroked his chin thoughtfully. "I remember living with my uncle in Scotland after my human parents died. He raised me for seven years before I went to live at the Northern Sanctuary. Apparently 'twas a deal my uncle made with the druids. They taught me about my powers and trained me. It wasn't until I was immortal that I became a Watcher in Scotland." Azrael paused, then added, "At least Erebus 'tis dead now."

A smile forced its way across my lips. "I will never forget the look on his face when you burst through the doors."

Azrael laughed. "I wasn't going to let you sacrifice yourself for us." He turned serious and lowered his voice. "You are too important. The Rebellion fears you and your powers."

I looked up at the night sky, hoping to see another shooting star. "I should have wished for something more practical than peace on Earth." I lowered my gaze. "It seems there will be no end to war, which means we will never have peace."

Azrael turned to me. "Take it from someone who has fought in many battles. Peace is not an end goal you achieve when everything is perfect in the world. It's something you claim when everything is perfect in your heart."

I knew he was right. It was just so hard to find peace in my heart after my foolish mistake with Erebus.

I gripped his hand tighter. "Now what is your wish?"

He lifted my hand and kissed it. The imprint of his lips seemed to linger on my skin. Azrael's words were soft, but powerfully sincere. "'Tis my deepest wish that you will allow me to court you formally." He paused and held my hand tighter as if he were afraid I would run away. "I want to marry you, Auriella. I've wanted this for hundreds of years."

The breath escaped my lungs. I swallowed fast and blinked several times. Why would an Immortal want to marry me? My body was fragile, weak, and would eventually die. My thoughts and emotions swam together like ingredients for a confusion potion. I desperately wanted to be with Azrael, but it would be the most tragic love story ever written.

"I can't," I managed to say past the pain of my aching heart. "I can't understand why you would even want me." I shook my head and squinted my eyes to keep from crying. "You are going to stay on Earth until Erebus is destroyed and I am going to grow old and die, just like the humans I protect."

"Aura, you are the most amazing person I have ever met." His voice was painfully genuine. "I will do anything to prove that one day I will be worthy to be your equal."

I pulled away from him. "You are immortal and—perfect. You don't have to prove anything to me." I twisted the reins around my fingers. "What will you do when I grow old and die?" I didn't wait for him to answer. "I don't know how Immortals cope with living year after year, watching the decades fade while everyone around them dies."

The memory of standing next to Lady Hannah's bedside overpowered my mind. Alwaien had taken my hand and led me to his mother's bedside. Lady Hannah's thin, white hair lay against her ashen face. Handing the ruby necklace to me, she said, "Thank you for giving me this necklace. It truly was a precious gift, but the longer I keep it, the more it becomes a curse. I can't live and watch everyone around me die."

"I can't live either!" I recalled falling to the ground and laying my head on her bed. My tears soaked the bedding as I gasped between sobs for painful breaths of air.

Lady Hannah had gripped my hand with amazing strength. Her words were fierce and powerful. "Auriella, you must live!"

I forced myself out of the nightmare and focused on the road ahead. "I can't think of a worse hell than living forever."

Azrael smiled, undeterred by my discouragement. "But I can think of no greater heaven than living with you for the rest of this life, and for the rest of eternity. The bonds of death won't break us, and the fire of hell will never take us." Azrael leaned closer. "Earth 'tis only a brief phase of our existence. Someday, whether we die or not, we will all go back to Neviah."

I tried to organize my swimming thoughts. "You see things so differently. I've never thought about what will happen to my Neviahan spirit when my human body dies."

Azrael let out a quick laugh. "Death can be hard, but 'tis not as bad as everyone thinks. If we die with honor, we go back to Neviah. Surprisingly, 'tis a lot like this world, but purer."

"Is this what the humans call heaven?" I couldn't help but wonder what happened to my loved ones after they died.

"There are many different heavens for humans. Everyone goes to the heaven where they feel most comfortable," Azrael answered. "Some humans even come to Neviah. The Great Kingdom of Neviah is a beautiful place." His eyes flickered with remembrance. "'Tis a crystal blue lake with all sorts of gems and shells at the bottom. When we get back, I will have to take you diving there again."

"Do you remember more of Neviah?" I desperately wished I could remember my home.

"Only faint glimpses," Azrael answered. "Unfortunately, most of my memories were veiled when I received my human body. But I retained one distinct memory."

"What is it?" I fervently anticipated any information about my home world.

Like an innate reaction, Azrael reached out and touched my fingers. A blue spark the size of a flame shot from my hand to his. He closed his hand around mine. "I remember you, Aura."

I hadn't expected that answer. "What was I like?"

Azrael's lips turned up and starlight danced in his eyes. "A lot like you are now." Azrael paused thoughtfully before he continued, "I want to stand by your side in the battles of this life and the perfect peace of the next. I love you, Aura." He swallowed hard. "Without you, I don't live—I only exist." His eyes glistened.

I looked down at his hands and remembered the way we connected when we created Starfire. Part of him would always be inside me now. No matter where I went or what I did, his energy would forever flow through me. I gasped at the inevitable thought of combining my soul with his again. At first the thought terrified me, but then filled me with delight.

I didn't know what to say for a long time.

The night slowly faded and the eastern horizon glowed with the promise of morning. There was so much I wanted to ask. I wanted to know what Erebus meant when he called Azrael the "fourth son of the Neviahan king" and "Brother." I needed to know about his dark years when he allied with the Shadow Legion.

Azrael finally broke the silence. "We have been traveling all night. Do you need to eat or rest?"

I shook my head. "Let's keep going."

"You are one determined lady," Azrael said, then added, "And one tough mortal."

A grin forced its way on my lips. "What about you? Do you need to sleep?" I asked.

Azrael shook his head. "'Twas enough storm last night for the wind to refuel my energy." He beamed brighter than the morning sun glistening off his dark hair. "You will have to marry me if you want to see me sleep."

"Azrael," I scolded. His playfulness lifted my spirits and made me melt. "I'm trying to have a serious conversation with you." I clenched my jaw and forced myself not to smile. "Do you ever sleep?" I managed to get out before I forgot my question.

"A little," he answered. "Sleeping 'tis more of a habit, and all habits can be broken."

I looked down at the raindrops glittering off the leaves and spring grass on the side of the road. It must be wonderful not having to sleep. I brushed the hair from my face. "It's one good thing I can see about being an Immortal." I unwrapped my wet cloak and wrung the cloth. A stream of cold water flowed onto the muddy road below.

Azrael narrowed his eyes and tilted his head. "What do you mean?"

"I have nightmares," I admitted. "Every night. I've had them since I was first attacked by a Shadow Wolf when I was thirteen. I see the most horrible things in my dreams. The only time I can rest is when I'm awake." I paused and waited for his reaction to my bizarre flaw.

"They are called Haunting Dreams." Azrael's voice softened sympathetically. "They come after very traumatic events."

I pressed my hand to my forehead. "I've tried everything to make them go away." I repressed the emotion flooding my voice. "I'm sure as an Immortal, all your nightmares happen while you are awake."

"All my dreams happen while I'm awake, too." Azrael looked at me with complete adoration. Love radiated like energy from his body. The wind brushed across my face and Azrael's eyes twinkled in that majestic way I loved.

The sky glowed with lavender, coral, and gold, along with all the other warm colors of morning light. As we reached the top of a hill, the taste of sea salt and brine flooded my senses. The endless ocean sparkled like liquid sapphires.

"Swansea," Azrael said. "'Tis the most beautiful thing I've ever seen." he paused, and a smile escaped his lips. His strong hands swallowed mine. "Well, almost the most beautiful thing I've ever seen."

Bittersweet emotions hit me at once. I longed to go to the Neviahan sanctuary, but I would miss the only home I knew.

I looked back to admire England one last time. Every shade of green painted itself across the rolling hills and ancient forests. The sun broke through the remaining clouds and streaked golden light across the kingdom.

A thud vibrated in my ears like the sea slamming into the shore. I coughed for air and leaned over the horse to brace myself. The taste of blood gushed into my mouth and pain screamed in every nerve of my body. I lifted my arm and stared at the dagger penetrating deep into my ribcage.

"Aura!" The horror in Azrael's voice frightened me.

My fingers stiffened like ice. I lost my grip and fell from the horse. Azrael snatched me as I dropped and laid me on the ground. The wooden handle protruded from my body. I strained to pull the weapon out of my chest.

"Hold still, Aura," Azrael's hoarse voice whispered.

The ground shook under us as horses approached.

I concentrated on breathing as I lay on the road. The sky spun above me as I sank into the cold mud. I blinked and fought to stay awake as energy left my body. It didn't matter how deep a breath I took—the air wouldn't stay in my lungs.

"You didn't think you would get out of England alive, did you?" a man's voice asked. "There's too high a price on your heads."

Baby growled and hovered over my body.

Azrael stood and formed his hands into fists.

The leader laughed and spoke in broken English. "One man? Against my assassins' guild?" He gestured toward many men in dark clothing descending from the woods. "You will die."

Azrael raised his hand and fire sprang from the ground in a defensive circumference around us.

The assassins stepped back from the flames that spontaneously burst to life.

The leader pointed at Azrael and snapped his fingers.

An assassin charged forward, raising his sword and shield. Azrael caught the edge of the blade in his hand and yanked it away. He whirled the weapon around and slid the sword into the assassin's armpit, then thrust the blade up and chopped off the attacker's arm.

Azrael spun the sword and severed the assassin's other arm at the shoulder. The shield and the arm fell to the ground.

All the assassins rushed toward Azrael at once. He unleashed his rage while hacking limbs, chopping through their line, and shattering their shields. He moved in a lethal dance of rage, barely touching the ground with his flawless footwork. Human blood soaked the ground and his clothes, but he still hadn't killed any of them.

The assassins retreated into the woods as blood spewed from their torsos where their arms had been.

The leader looked at the limbs littering the ground. His eyes bulged with terror. He reached for his throwing knives—their handles matched the one protruding from my chest. Azrael hurled his sword. The sunlight glinted off the long blade propelling through the air.

Azrael's blade broke through the assassin's skull and pinned his head to the ground several yards away. Everything was a blur and moved in slow motion.

Azrael's knees hit the muddy road beside me. He embraced me in his arms, "No! No!" The mud turned deep crimson around him. He pulled the dagger from my chest as my dangerous blood ran down his arm and dripped off his elbow.

I had lost too much blood and I could barely speak, let alone summon fire to heal myself. I looked into his eyes and knew I wasn't going to live. I had to say it or I would regret it for the rest of eternity.

"Azrael." It took all my strength to whisper his name. I blinked several times to bring his face back into focus. I met his celestial gaze and said with the last of my strength, "I love you, Azrael."

My body went limp in his arms as my vision faded to a single point. The last thing I saw was his black mask hitting the earth.

The curse shattered into sparkling black dust.

Chapter Nineteen

New Life

Dying wasn't as bad as I thought it would be. The worst feeling was leaving Azrael behind in emotional agony over my death. The mortal wound that claimed my life didn't even hurt as much as other wounds I'd had. Death was merciful. After the initial pain of the strike, I just got cold, then fell asleep.

I no longer felt tired, but alert and full of energy as I watched white mist swirl around me. It seemed a little like the heaven humans talk about.

The sun shone in every direction, creating a bright world of serenity. There had to be more than just white clouds and sunlight. Where was the Kingdom of Neviah? Was I stuck in this whitewash forever?

A hand reached through the veil of clouds as if beckoning me.

"Hello?" I tried to see his face through the cloud bank. "I am looking for Neviah," I said, not knowing how this stranger could help me.

"Who seeks Neviah?" he asked. His voice was kind and familiar.

"I am Auriella, the Lady of Neviah."

"You're early." The stranger's voice sounded more lighthearted.

I relaxed. "Yes—not by choice, I assure you."

The stranger laughed and reached out for my hand. I took it and he pulled me through the clouds into the sun.

I immediately recognized the stranger as if I had known him all my life. The King of Neviah's face shone with white light. His eyes emanated pure love and joy.

The king put his arm around me. "That was a pretty tough fight, Auriella."

"You're telling me," I said sheepishly. "Orion warned me I would fall off my horse."

The king laughed in a warm baritone tones. He looked like a slightly older version of his fourth son, Azrael.

Now that my mind was no longer veiled, the king and I picked up right where we left off. I basked in our familiar relationship and his gentle fatherly love.

Three silver moons dotted the bright pastel sky of my home world. A garden of crystal flowers surrounded us. Warm rainbow snowflakes fell from the sky and soaked into the ground.

"I am so happy to be home." I took in a deep breath and absorbed the beauty. I noticed an aqua-blue lake glittering like a sea of treasure next to the majestic ivory palace. "There's the lake Azrael told me about."

"It was one of my son's favorite places," the king said. He pointed to a waterfall pouring waves and mist into the lake. "And that was one of your favorite places."

Memories returned, rushing over me. "There is a crystal cave behind the falls," I remembered out loud.

The king nodded.

"Azrael and I used to swim into the cave and . . ." I stopped speaking. I remembered the feeling of water-soaked Neviahan cloth glistening against my body as I waited for Azrael in our secret cave. I recalled pulling my knees to my chest, watching the water for him.

Azrael had emerged from the hidden tunnel leading from the lake to our cave. Water flooded over his body, making him glisten like the gems we discovered in the lake. Our gem bag was slung across his bare chest. I took in the memory of his face, before the curse mask shamed his beautiful features. His body was strong, but not nearly as battle-sculpted as it had become after years of combat on Earth.

Even in my memory, I couldn't glance away from his broad smile. Azrael pulled the bag over his head and set it on the crystal cave floor.

I eagerly knelt beside him. "Did we find the Star Diamond?" I asked.

Azrael opened the bag. "Not this time."

I dropped my shoulders. "The star showers only happened once every ten thousand years. We might be sent to Earth before the next event."

Azrael pulled shells, pearls, uncut agates, and pink sapphires from the bag. He placed an angel shell in my hand. My skin tingled with energy when we touched. Azrael put his arm around me and kissed my cheek. "For my angel."

I admired the smooth shell as it emanated light. "Do you think there'll be things like this on Earth?"

Azrael shrugged. "If the Rebellion doesn't destroy the planet before we get there."

I set the shell aside and turned to Azrael. "Promise you'll find me on Earth," I pleaded. "No matter what happens."

Azrael smiled and brushed back my hair. "Of course I will."

I wasn't convinced. "Azrael, what if we are sent to different countries? What if we are sent at different time periods? What happens when all your pre-Earth memories fade? How will you find me then?"

Azrael looked me in the eyes. "My love, I hope you don't worry this much when we get to Earth."

Azrael pulled me close to him. "If we are sent to different countries, I will travel whatever distance it takes to get to you. If we are sent to different time periods, I will become an Immortal and wait for you until you are born into your human body. And if all my pre-Earth memories fade, I promise, I will never forget you. Our energies will combine and remind us of who we are." I relaxed in his arms. Azrael kissed my forehead then said, "It's our destiny to be together, and I will embrace that destiny with all my heart. "Nothing can break us, and the fires of hell will never take us."

Energy blanketed us in a swirling cocoon of fire and wind. Azrael leaned forward, and his lips caressed mine in a kiss both passionate and pure. I ran my fingers through his hair as he pressed me closer to him. Fire and wind rushed through our souls like a dance of dedication and love. Our powers fed off each other, growing in strength. The light of our love reflected off every gem and crystal in the cave.

I gasped for breath and pulled myself from the pre-Earth memory of Azrael. No wonder we felt the way we did on Earth. We had connected so many times before. Though our minds were veiled, our souls still remembered, our hearts yearned to be whole again, and our energy fought to combine as one.

I looked away from the waterfall and cast my gaze to the ivory castle and silver city. "Now that my human body is destroyed, I won't be able to see Azrael again until the war is over."

"Your human body wasn't completely destroyed," the King of Neviah said. "Your heart was still intact."

"Are you saying I can go back?" I asked. I wanted to return to Azrael, but knew that meant going back into battle and leaving this perfect peace.

The king nodded. "Yes, you can return, but things will be different if you go back. In the few moments you have been in here Neviah, many years have gone by on Earth. Erebus has regained his strength and is preparing an assault against the Northern Sanctuary."

"He's alive?" I dropped my head in my hand and realized, "The necklace. That's how he survived. Please forgive me," I begged the king. "I let him have it."

"You did the right thing," the king said.

I furrowed my brow. "How could giving Erebus a healing necklace be the right thing?"

"Erebus has grown confident in the trinket's ability, but the magic of the necklace is weakening. By giving him the necklace, you have set the only trap that could ensnare him. You and Azrael can defeat him. Your strengths and powers are enhanced when you are with each other."

I looked back at our waterfall across the lake. "As wonderful as Neviah is, it won't be heaven without Azrael."

The king looked pleased, but unsurprised, like he already knew the choice I would make. "Down at the bottom of the lake there is a magnificent sword—the Sword of Neviah."

I remembered the king's sword from the pre-Earth battle against Erebus and the rebels.

"This sword can only be used by one who has the power of Starfire. It can cut through any object, no matter how dense. The blade will never dull, chip, or rust. It can even pierce through that which is intangible, such as the Spirits of Shadow, before they have a chance to take human bodies and become Shadow Lords. This weapon will give you a tremendous advantage in the war on Earth. The Sword of Neviah is just as immortal as the North Star, and it's yours, Auriella." The king motioned toward the lake.

"Mine?" I couldn't believe he was giving me his own sword, the very weapon that defeated Erebus in the pre-Earth battle.

"I will miss you, Lady Auriella." He opened his arms to hug me. "When you go back to Earth, don't forget who you are and how important you are to the kingdom."

I threw my arms around him. "I will miss you too. I promise I will always remember."

His lips pulled up into a smile. "When the war is over, the whole kingdom will celebrate your victorious return." He motioned toward the tranquil aqua lake where the Sword of Neviah lay.

I stepped to the shore and dove into the water.

Calm liquid enveloped me. I couldn't help but compare how different it was to the water on Earth. I easily swam through the light water as if it were air. As I swam deeper, the water never suffocated me with its dense pressure. Even as I reached the bottom of the lake, the white sun glistened off every shell and gem.

I ran my fingers through the silver sand, searching for the sword. A stream of bubbles trickled from the lakebed and pink pearls floated buoyantly from the stream of air.

I swam toward the pocket of air.

There it was. The king's magnificent sword stood out among the pearls and made even the silver sand seem dull as it radiated light.

The handle of the weapon spiraled like a unicorn's horn. Swirling white flames were etched into the hand guard and woven around the handle. Light reflected from the sword, making everything around me shimmer.

I reached through the weightless water, gripped the handle of the sword, and pulled it from the sand.

I swam toward the surface and emerged from the water. I took in a breath of air and blinked my eyes open as if I had just awoken.

The lake was gone. The world around me seemed dark and cold. I was back on Earth.

I lay on my back, surrounded in volcanic cinders as I stared up at the North Star in the night sky.

In my mind I replayed my death and brief moment in Neviah with the king, determined not to forget those memories.

Flames lapped over me in gentle waves. I stood and gripped the handle of the king's sword. Red flames swirled around me and down the blade.

Except for the ash covering my new body, I was naked. Steam billowed off my skin in white waves. My sparkling ivory feet made no sound and left no footprint as I stepped from the pyre.

Like the Phoenix, I had been reborn—this time as one of the Immortals.

About the Author

Deirdra (pronounced: Dare-dra) has traveled the country as an Amazon Best Selling author and speaker. Her books have sold worldwide to a variety of audiences. She writes theological fantasy, organizational self help, true crime, and fiction for children in trauma. Deirdra is the founder of Eden Literary Foundation which is dedicated to printing, gathering, and distributing donated books to children in the foster care system, military personnel and their families, and victims of gender targeted crimes.

Find Deirdra Online:

www.DeirdraEden.com

www.Knightess.com

www.HerEden.com

www.EdenLiterary.com

FREE Watchers Coloring Book

The Watchers Series
Coloring Book

By Author and Illustrator
Deirdra Eden

For a Free Copy of The Watchers Coloring Book, visit

https://www.smashwords.com/books/view/429719

and enter coupon code AZ54J

Made in the USA
Las Vegas, NV
11 January 2022

41083343R10174